POWER IN THE BLOOD

A JOHN JORDAN MYSTERY BOOK 1

MICHAEL LISTER

PULPWOOD PRESS

COPYRIGHT

Power in the Blood (Revised 2020)
Written by Michael Lister
Introduction by Michael Connelly

Large Print Edition ISBN: 978-1-947606-45-6

(John Jordan Novels)
Power in the Blood
Blood of the Lamb
Flesh and Blood
(Special Introduction by Margaret Coel)

The Body and the Blood
Double Exposure
Blood Sacrifice
Rivers to Blood
Burnt Offerings
Innocent Blood
(Special Introduction by Michael Connelly)
Separation Anxiety
Blood Money
Blood Moon
Thunder Beach
Blood Cries
A Certain Retribution
Blood Oath
Blood Work
Cold Blood
Blood Betrayal
Blood Shot
Blood Ties
Blood Stone
Blood Trail
Bloodshed
Blue Blood
And the Sea Became Blood
The Blood-Dimmed Tide
Blood and Sand

<u>Cold Blood</u>
<u>Blood Shot</u>

(Love Stories)
<u>Carrie's Gift</u>

(Short Story Collections)
North Florida Noir
Florida Heat Wave
Delta Blues
Another Quiet Night in Desperation

(The Meaning Series)
<u>Meaning Every Moment</u>
<u>The Meaning of Life in Movies</u>

INTRODUCTION BY THE
AUTHOR

I became a writer in the summer of 1994.

Three years and three months later, in the fall of 1997, I became a published author.

During this time, two true crime cases dominated our culture, the public national trial that was the O. J. Simpson case and the horrific, tragic death of JonBenét Ramsey—both of which are experiencing renewed interest as I write this, because they too are marking their twentieth anniversary.

Power in the Blood was my very first attempt at writing a novel—not just my first novel to be published, but the first I ever wrote.

Writing is like anything else—you learn

by doing, by practice. I've been practicing the craft of writing for nearly twenty-three years now. In that time I've gotten better at it, grown and evolved, discovered my voice, honed my style.

After twenty-plus years of writing, the *Power in the Blood* I would write today is not the *Power in the Blood* that was published twenty years ago. Of course, if I hadn't written that *Power in the Blood* back then, I wouldn't be able to write *Cold Blood*, the novel I'm working on as I write this. Way leads to way. Book leads to book. Everything builds on that which comes before.

The writer I am today is only because of the writers I was before.

How did I become that first fledgling writer?

I was probably born with a love of story. I can certainly remember craving story as a child. Being moved by story are among my earliest memories.

As a teenager who was reading mostly nonfiction, I was led to detective fiction by, of all things, a TV show. *Spenser for Hire* led me to the books by Robert B. Parker the show was based on, and I fell in love with character, prose, and dialog.

After high school, I moved from my small Florida Panhandle town of Wewahitchka to Atlanta—not unlike John Jordan—and though I was there for theological training, it was a lit class taught by Tricia Weeks that was to be among the most inspirational and influential of my undergraduate degree program.

Then I happened upon the 1990 Avenel edition of G. K. Chesterton's *Father Brown Crime Stories* in a dusty old bookstore in Atlanta the year I graduated from theology college and was ordained, and it was nothing less than serendipitous. During that momentous year of transition, as I was being born into my adult life, Chesterton in many ways became my literary father, and Brown the fictional father to my ecclesiastical sleuth, John Jordan.

Between 1988 and 1994, I attempted on and off to write short stories and screenplays, but it wouldn't be until the summer of '94, as I was finishing my graduate degree in theology and about to enter into full-time prison chaplaincy, that I became a writer. That summer, in an upstairs room at my parents' house I converted into my library and study because my small home didn't have room for them, in the semi-coolness provided by the inefficient window unit, after a long and drawn-out delivery, a writer was born. John Jordan was born. This book was born.

It was during this time that I discovered other crime writers who have had a profound influence on my work, like James Lee Burke and Michael Connelly (who has contributed an essay for this book). It was also during this time that I attended my first novel-writing workshop taught by Lynn Wallace (who has also contributed an essay for this book).

And because way leads to way and book leads to book, I began a kind of self-designed curriculum for my education as a new writer, which included Shakespeare, Hemingway, Dostoevsky, Tolstoy, Melville, Chandler, Faulkner, Flannery O'Connor, Updike, Roth, Irving, DeLillo, Fitzgerald, and Cormac McCarthy.

Over the next twenty-plus years, I continued my education and training, and after some thirty books, thirteen of which are John Jordan novels, here I am.

I feel like somewhere along the way I learned to write some, and I hope twenty years from now I'll have learned a lot more.

At some point during the past twenty years since *Power in the Blood* was first published, probably back around the time I learned a little about writing, I began wanting to rewrite it. I've thought about it for years, but was uncertain as to how to approach it or when to take the time away from current and future books to do it. And then a couple of years back it occurred to me that the twentieth anniversary of the book would be the perfect time.

The moment I decided to rewrite *Power in the Blood* for this special edition, I had to decide exactly what that meant. Was I going to toss out the original and start over? Was I going to keep the original and just tweak and lightly edit? Was I going to change the story? The plot? The style?

Ultimately, I chose to keep the original book, but do heavy revision without changing the essential plot and characters in any fundamental way.

This new, revised version of *Power in the Blood* more closely matches my style, my voice, my approach to the novel today than the original version from twenty years ago. However, since I kept the characters, plot, and structure of the original, this new version is a hybrid—neither completely the novel I would have written back then, nor the one I would write today.

This is a remodel instead of new construction. I kept the bones of the original book, the foundation, some of the wiring, walls, and plumbing, but rebuilt and repurposed and redid most everything else. This new version is not a completely new house, but neither is it an old one either. In that way, I believe it shows the first-time novelist I was *and* the twenty-sixth-time novelist I've become.

The writer I've become has increasingly been about what I leave out as much as what I put in. Saying more, evoking more, discovering more with less—fewer words, less exposition, less explanation—has been the biggest part of my particular evolution. And this new version of *Power in the Blood* reflects that. Whatever else it is, it's cleaner, leaner prose, and closer to my authentic style, my true voice.

I hope you enjoy this version of *Power in the Blood*, that it serves as a good introduction to John Jordan. And, most importantly of all, I hope you see in it the seeds of what the series will become and want to journey with John throughout the entirety of the books featuring him, however many books that ultimately turns out to be.

Michael Lister

January 2017

MICHAEL CONNELLY
INTRODUCTION

It's hard to write a book. You have to keep so many plates spinning on sticks. You've got the plot. You've got the place you are writing about. You've got the what-happens-next plate that can never wobble. You've got the momentum plate. You've got the humor plate. And the compassion plate. And I could go on and on. You've got the need to blend all of these things together into one act and keep them spinning, always spinning. Oh, and did I mention that you are holding all of these sticks up and spinning all of these plates while walking on a tight rope? No, wait, walking would be too easy. Change that. You are actually riding a tricycle on a tight rope.

Yes, it's a major high wire act, fraught with danger and failure, and that wire is the most important part of the whole thing. That high wire is character, and the whole thing comes crashing down plates and all if you don't have it right. If that wire is not taut and reliable and secure. If that character is not one for the ages.

Now with all of that, think about getting back on that high wire with the same character time and time again. Six shows a week and two on Sunday. It is not for the faint of heart, I can tell you that. It is hard to do it once. It is harder to do it time and time again. And that's what writing a book series is like.

And that is what Michael Lister has done for 20 years with the character of John Jordan and what he has been able to do for 20 years with his own muse. Not just sustain. Not just keep his balance on the wire. Not just go back to the well again and again. He has filled the well, he has expanded the boundaries of what he does with character. He has gotten better. He has somehow been able to find within him the inspiration to get back on the wire and do it again, only better.

It may be that the challenge and accomplishment of this can only be fully known and understood by the one who does it. No matter. Take my word for it. Michael Lister has become a master storyteller in his first 20 years and he's only getting started.

Michael Connelly

January 2017

REAL BLOOD: JOHN JORDAN AND HIS COUNTERPART

B y Aaron Bearden

IF YOU ARE READING THIS, it is possible you count yourself as a John Jordan fan. Perhaps you have followed him through all of his cases, navigating crimes both real and fictional across several towns and multiple states, through ups and downs in his personal life.

You may be a casual admirer of Mr. Jordan's, one who has read a few stories about him, but are still working your way through all twelve (and counting!) novels in his series. Should time allow, you may get caught up on them before too many more are published, turning your reading list into a Sisyphean endeavor—albeit a very satisfying and noble one.

You may have followed him for years, awaiting each new book with the polite patience only a dedicated lover of art anticipating the next foray into the unknown territory of a favorite artist's mind can know, and finishing it in less time than it took for the font of the title on the cover to be selected (not that there's anything wrong with that).

There is a slim chance you have enjoyed reading about John Jordan for twenty years now, having started with Power in the Blood upon its release in 1997. If you have remained a member of Michael Lister's audience throughout, know that you share in something rare in any artistic medium: a twenty-year relationship between artist and audience is not something that happens often to either party.

There is also the chance this is your first time reading a John Jordan mystery. On

Michael's behalf, I welcome you to his literary world, and hope it will not be your only excursion therein.

I say all of that to explain that I, in comparison to most every reader I have met at one of Michael's signings, am a relative newcomer to the character of John Jordan.

When I first met Michael, Power in the Blood was his only John Jordan novel.

When I finally got around to reading one, there were ten.

It's not that I didn't read any of Michael's work in that time. On the contrary, I had read all of the Jimmy Riley "Big" books, Double Exposure, Cataclysmos, and several non-series titles. I had narrated the audiobook for Meaning Every Moment, and produced several other audiobooks for him. We had worked on a play (The Big Hello) and a short film (Spilled Blood). I was well acquainted with the Listerverse.

Except for that John Jordan guy.

I can't say what had ever kept me from reading one. I had meant to. Like the dinner guests in Luis Bunuel's The Discreet Charm of the Bourgeoisie, who had every intention of sitting down to enjoy a meal together but kept getting interrupted, I was always finding something standing in my way, blocking the path. Sometimes it was another of Michael's projects on which I was working. Sometimes it was one of my own.

The first time I reached the last page of a John Jordan book, I knew what the readers I had met at Michael's signings had felt, some for the fourth, fifth, or maybe tenth time. I had been treated to something special. It was no ordinary yarn.

I say "yarn" because, in some sense, that's the foundation of the novel as an art form. It very often can be boiled down to a novelist saying, "Hey, let me tell you this story I thought up. I think you'll like it." There are certain required elements: a setting, a plot, a protagonist. All those things you learned in English or theater classes. The rest, very often, is just a measure of how well it's dressed up and presented.

What I felt when reading a John Jordan book was something else. It was a chance to observe an author so in touch with his character—his creation—that it transcended the flea circus of storytelling. I felt like I was reading about a real person.

John Jordan is not a cookie-cutter carica-
ture. He's not a brooding loner, too devoted
to the job to ever have time for a family. He
doesn't play by his own rules. He's not a
loose cannon, above the law, with a death
wish, or in possession of any other silly trait
that lesser characters rely on to seem interesting.

John is principled. Dedicated. Compassionate. Loyal and honest.

Yet for all his virtues, John's flaws are
what make him three-dimensional. He is un-
wavering in his pursuit of what's right, but he
doubts himself when it comes to those to
whom he is closest. He reminds himself to be
understanding with the woman he loves. He
worries about the choices he makes as a parent. He's had his moments of weakness.
Sometimes those moments lasted longer
than he'd want to admit.

I believe one way to know if a character is
well-written is if you, the reader or audience,
feel as though you know how they would
react to situations that aren't on the page. We
know enough about John Jordan to know
where he would stand. He advocates for the
oppressed, the downtrodden, and the mis-

treated. He has an obligation to justice, but not to revenge. He makes a case for truth, not speculation. We know this about John because Michael has presented us with a character so well fleshed-out that we know not just his actions, but his reasons for them.

I don't want to spoil details of any specific books for anyone who hasn't read them. I wouldn't dream of robbing from anyone the discoveries that wait in the pages of the John Jordan series.

There is little I could offer to long-time readers of the series anyway, regarding the character.

If I have anything to tell you now, on the twentieth anniversary of John Jordan's existence as a literary hero of the people, it is probably best summarized in eight words.

Readers know John Jordan; I know Michael Lister.

The reason John Jordan is such a complex, compelling figure is that he comes from the brain—or the soul—of a complex and compelling person. Michael Lister exhibits many (most? all?) of John's positive qualities. He is compassionate, principled, loyal, and honest.

Yet I don't believe for a moment that John is a product of wish fulfillment, or a manifestation of Michael himself on the page. That is the province of bad writers, who write themselves into a story to defeat the villain and save the girl.

As I said I met Michael when Power in the Blood was his only John Jordan book, around 1999 or 2000. He was a guest speaker in a writing course I was taking, and having already published a hardcover novel, he was something of a guru to the class.

His hometown and mine are a fifteen-minute drive apart. Without realizing it, as a child I rode by his family home every week. It wasn't until ten years later that we would meet, and ten after that before we became friends. In that time I had released an album and felt comfortable enough with my work to think I could talk to him without bothering him, or sounding like I was asking for advice or help.

We became friends while I produced an audiobook for him. We bonded over a shared appreciation for art, especially music and film. We have overlapping but not identical tastes, and have introduced each other to new favorite books, songwriters, TV shows, and so on.

At this point if a day goes by without speaking to him at least through a text, it feels wrong.

I know enough of Michael to know John Jordan is not merely how he wants to see himself. If anything, John is how Michael wants to see us all. He wants to see John's integrity and devotion in everyone. He wants the world around him to be filled with people who will do what's right, even when it's not what's easiest. He wants to know the person behind him in line at the grocery store or driving ahead of him on the road is as mindful of how they live their life and as concerned about the choices they make as a father, mother, spouse, neighbor, or friend as John is.

Some writers want to be like their characters. I think Michael wants us all to be like John.

I had the opportunity to interview Michael at a release party for one of his books, and we spent over an hour with an audience of loyal readers, discussing his projects. When our time was up, there was one question left that I didn't get a chance to ask.

When you wrote Power in the Blood, how much did you know about John Jordan, compared to what you know about him after twenty years and ten books?

I suspect I know the answer to that question now.

In that time, Michael has raised three amazing kids. He has married a woman who makes him happier than any person I know. He has seen his career take off, thanks in no small part to John Jordan. He has had wonderful opportunities, to interact with fans, befriend some of his favorite writers, and live every day translating the ideas in his head into various books, plays, and films, surrounded by a group of friends and family he treasures. He lives with the integrity of his characters and an awareness and thankfulness for the moment he's in at all times.

Michael has always known the person he is, but the past twenty years have given him chances to live up to his ideals and display his own character; he's also always known the core of who John is, but has had twenty years to test him by putting him into trying situations and sending him down some dark roads. Today, both men have come through more confident, more whole.If I had to guess, I'd say Michael has learned almost as much about John in the past twenty years as he's learned about himself.

And that, my friends, can mean nothing but good things for us, the patient readers anxiously waiting for the thirteenth, fifteenth, or even twentieth John Jordan book, and beyond.

To Michael Lister I would say thank you, for so many things.

To you, the reader, I would also say thank you, on Michael's behalf. Each and every one of you is appreciated greatly, I know. Your enthusiasm for his work drives him to create.

Here's to another twenty years of John Jordan, and may we all be a little more like him in our own way.

AARON BEARDEN
11/30/16

LAND OF BLOOD AND HONEY

B y Enrique Fernández

I KNEW a guy once who whenever he was asked where he was from would reply, "Grover's Corner." To anyone who didn't figure out the ruse, it sounded familiar, except that, where was that town? It was, it is, Thornton Wilder's fiction from his famous play Our Town. I had the same experience with the town in the first John Jordan novel by Michael Lister. Pottersville. I knew that place. Why, I think I've been there. Many times.

Usually around Christmas. Pottersville is what Frank Capra calls his also fictional Bedford Falls in the film It's a Wonderful Life when the angel shows a suicidal George Bailey what his hometown would become if he'd never existed, a nightmare town filmed using all the atmospheric tricks of film noir. What better name for a town in a violent crime thriller like Power in the Blood, the first John Jordan novel that, like Capra's movie, deals with the transcendent theme of redemption?

Twenty years into the John Jordan series about a crime-solving prison chaplain, Lister no longer fictionalizes the town's name, his own hometown, but calls it by the unpronounceable Wewahitchka. It was in Wewa, as everyone calls it, that I met Michael Lister's work and the author himself. An article in a local electric company mailer told me about a crime novel set in the town, written by a Wewahitchka writer of some renown, though unknown to me. I read it.

Wewahitchka, a one-streetlight town in the Florida Panhandle, had already enjoyed its fifteen minutes of fame, in Ullee's Gold, a 1997 film by Victor Nuñez, who sets all his work in the Panhandle, starring Peter Fonda in an award-winning role as a Wewa bee-keeper—the town is home to artisanal Tupelo honey. Many scenes were filmed locally. But Lister, born into a well-established Wewa family, goes deeper. For me, the thrill of reading A Certain Retribution, the Lister novel I first encountered, was how everything happened in places I knew: the bar, once a bikers' hangout called, precisely, The Bar, but now renamed and less raffish; the houseboats on the river; the one coffee shop in town, where Lister gives himself a cameo appearance. It was not a John Jordan book, but it was certainly a crime thriller, set right here in my new hometown.

I had moved to Wewa after living in New York City and Miami, both cities where I worked as a journalist, the doomed profession of our times. When the doom caught up with me, and being of retirement age, I figured it was time to retreat from worldly noise and finally try my hand at what Michael Lister was doing at a much younger age and with great success: writing books. My sister had married a local man and lived in his family property outside Wewa, a small ranch where they raised horses and chickens. My aging parents had moved right next door, into a double-wide trailer the size of a comfortable suburban home, and my father had died there. I lived with my mom the last two years of her life and now the double-wide—common housing in these parts—was my home.

The Florida Panhandle is the Deep South, as Lister himself has made clear, unlike South Florida, where one is hard pressed to hear a Southern accent. "The best fiction is regional, is geographically specific," Lister has said, calling himself "one of those novelists" of the romantic and misery-ridden South. Like the scent of honeysuckle in The Sound and the Fury, the heady perfume of the region haunts, underpinned by an extroverted religiosity—so different from the tight Protestantism of the old North—and a painful history. This is a zone where crime could be rightfully called sin, where a chaplain, a prison official whose job is to redeem rather than punish, is the right kind of hero.

John Jordan enters the world witnessing

a killing, and then, in a grotesque bit of slap-stick, falling into the victim and soaking up his blood. But he's cool. The chaplain takes his role seriously and takes control of the situation. He is, after all, a man of God. And he's also a detective, solving, as they all must, crimes—which is to say, riddles. Mysteries. And mysteries are what crime fiction and religion are both all about. Except that in one, what matters is to eliminate the mysteries and let the light shine through, while in the other the light shines through when there's faith in the mysteries. A detective/chaplain, who else could manage both?

At the core of the John Jordan mysteries is the region itself. This Deep South in North Florida. There is mystery here. The woods are thick with undergrowth. Trek for a while and they become wetlands. If Florida's most famous wetland, the Everglades, is a flat and endless savanna of sawgrass, the swamps here are bayous, just as wet but denser. And there's none of the genteel South of lore. No antebellum mansions until you're practically in Georgia. Instead, the improvised life of double-wide trailers and riverboats. Sub-urban ranch houses. Beach houses on stilts.

Cottages from an Old Florida that has not yet fully succumbed to development.

Wewahitchka/Pottersville is a town with practically no fast food chains or other signs of the tacky modernity of the Sun Belt. Yet, there isn't any small-town cuteness either, gussied up for tourists. To say everyone knows everyone is no exaggeration. Or as I've heard it said, "Everyone here knows a girl is pregnant before the girl herself finds out." Homes don't need to be locked, and instead of police presence, everybody has guns. Not that they're shooting one another, except in Michael Lister's novels. Extreme politeness, that Southern trait, is extended to everyone, of every background. There is a black section of town, "the quarters," mentioned in Power in the Blood. In private conversation you'll hear the notorious N-word, but you're more likely to hear the r-word, from folk who rightfully belong to that group, as "redneck" is used sometimes with humorous pride and sometimes as the identity of those who exhibit ignorance and crassness, coming from the lips of those who in gentler circumstances apply the word to themselves and their kind.

But none of this is obvious. It took my reading Lister's novels to begin to unravel the mysteries of the world I now live in. I knew there was a prison outside of town, but I'd never been in it. I hadn't spent time in the local bars until Michael and his wife Dawn invited me for an evening out and I heard them both harmonizing on a country song since it was karaoke night. And though my brother-in-law is as local as they come, I'm as outsider as they come—hell, I'm a foreigner. I wanted to learn more, and these violent yet spiritual stories set in what was now my environment were enriching my understanding.

Were I homegrown like Lister, I'd certainly be writing about this region and this town; in fact, this essay is a hopefully not too clumsy attempt to do so. And I'd be drawn to the religious dimension, as he is. It's not just that Wewa and environs have churches of all Protestant denominations, from lofty Episcopalian to the occasional tent revival. It's the blood, the word that occurs, in typical fashion for crime series, in the title of every John Jordan book. The blood of crime, that which soaks the chaplain detective in the very first pages of Power in the Blood, but most importantly the blood of sacrament.

Sacrament, sacrifice. If these stories that probe religious depths are violent, it's because Christianity is violent at its core, even if at its core it preaches peace. It's based on the barbaric torture and execution of an innocent man, and it considers itself the continuation and renewal of another faith that has as its story the execution of an innocent, prevented when God stays the hand of Abraham about to slay his son. Both were sacrifices, the snuffing of life with a religious purpose. What is the purpose, then, of the violence around us? Lister's detective chaplain struggles to learn the truths of whodunits and of the relationship of man, that violent creature, to God.

The first struggle requires powers of detection, as well as personal bravery. The second gets no help from detection, for it's an undetectable mystery that can only be approached through sacrament and sacrifice, through the power in the blood. And though there is no answer, there is, there can be, redemption. A prison is, after all, a house of sinners. Who could possibly be in more need of salvation?

But Jordan is no ascetic saint. He has struggled with alcoholism. He is wildly attracted to women. And he certainly doesn't see the world through rose-tinted lenses. As Lister has pointed out, he breaks from the genteel tradition of religious detective fiction (Father Brown) and moves instead into the hard-boiled genre. Yet, all the characters in the novels, even the worst, are human. No cardboard villains.

Lister takes me by the hand and introduces them to me. As of this writing I have yet to read all the John Jordan stories, never mind the others, for he is a prolific writer. And, as I discover the more I read, he's a craftsman of his trade and a deep one. Crime fiction can be unabashed entertainment—in fact, to be good, it should always be that—but it can go to the same places literary fiction does: a meditation through writing on the human, the divine, the social, the sacred, the role of humans in history and vice versa, the attraction of the concrete, and the unavoidable pull, due to the confluence of mortality and consciousness, of the metaphysical.

I navigate the blood—always shed by crime and always participating in sacrament —that flows through the John Jordan books like the river that flows by Wewahitchka. Drive through here and you wouldn't know this is a river town, a magnet for fishing enthusiasts. Like so much about Wewa, the river is hidden. You have to follow the little road signs that point to a boat dock, and after a short drive through backcountry, there's the river. The mystery. "The river is within us," TS Eliot wrote. Unlike Lister, I am not from this town, from this river. But reading him, I begin to feel it flowing within me.

A NOTE ABOUT SETTING

Note: This novel is set in the mid '90s and the cell phone and video camera technology or lack thereof reflects that time.

1

I was standing at the gate of Potter Correctional Institution staring at him when he was killed.

Waiting to be buzzed into the pedestrian sally port, my view slightly impaired by the chain-link fence and razor wire, I was gazing into the back of a trash truck.

The hot July sun reflected off the razors like the mirrored shades of a redneck police chief, waves of heat dancing through circles of steel, and the air was thick and difficult to breathe.

The clear, blue, cloudless sky offered no shelter from the sun's assault, nor any

promise of rain for the parched planet beneath my feet.

I had no idea what I was witnessing at
the time. A murder? An accident? A suicide?

At first, all I could see was a young correctional officer with a bad complexion and
wide hips standing on the back of a white
Ford flatbed pickup truck, thrusting a long
metal rod into the trash bags piled on it.

His hips were so wide and strangely
shaped, it looked like he was wearing football
pants with full pads. Sweat poured off his
face, and his light brown uniform was soaked
through. It wasn't the young officer's odd appearance but the enthusiasm with which he
executed his task that caught my attention.

I was awestruck by the violent blows
each bag received.

Obviously there were more effective and
efficient ways to search the trash before it
was removed from the institution, which
meant the manner in which he was doing it
was a warning to all the inmates looking on
as much as it was any kind of actual hunt for
an inmate trying to escape.

Like a prehistoric sign language or an antiquated form of Morse code, every violent stab was a character of communication. Taken together, they sent out a concise message for all who had the eyes to see—attempting to escape PCI in the back of a trash truck was a bad idea.

Even though inmates were sometimes treated like trash and at times acted like trash, they were not going to escape by pretending to be trash.

What a strange, surreal little claustrophobic world I was entering.

It wasn't that I didn't understand the need for a certain type of security. I did.

And I knew an officer had to check every vehicle and everything in those vehicles before they left the institution. Recalling just one of the many real-life horror stories of escaped inmates recited during my recent new-employee orientation was more than enough to convince me of that.

But I couldn't help but believe that the excessiveness expressed in this particular brutal method of searching the trash contributed to the violent and essentially inhumane environment of this secret and closed society.

Preparing to stab the final bag in the center of the truck, the officer stumbled over the outer ones and hovered above it. Raising the weapon above his head, he brought it down with a force far more incredible than even the others had been.

But this time when the rod entered the bag there was a deep thump, followed by the sound similar to that of twigs caught in a lawn mower.

This time the metal implement did not return when the officer attempted to retract it.

He then took another stance and yanked even harder.

On his third attempt in that position he pulled it free, ripping open the bag as he did. It was dripping with blood.

At first, I thought he had stabbed a can of chocolate syrup from Food Services or an old oil can from Maintenance, but his reaction quickly convinced me otherwise.

The young officer lost all color and stumbled backward, dropping his blunt spear, and reached for his radio only to discover that it wasn't there—something that served to make him only more frantic.

I waved to the officer in the control room, who immediately buzzed me in.

As I ran in, the officer on the flatbed began yelling.

"Oh God. Chaplain. Chaplain. Chaplain, get out here now. Call for help. Get—" His voice, which had been weak and tight and frightened, turned to pure high-pitched hysteria.

"Oh God . . . Oh God . . . What the . . . Oh shit . . . There's a body in the . . ." With that, he passed out.

I rushed over to the second gate that led into the vehicle sally port, and before I reached it, the control room had already buzzed it open. I ran straight through the gate, pausing on the other side only long enough to close it behind me.

Heart hammering in my chest, thoughts a blur of indistinguishable images. Climbing up onto the back of the truck, I saw that the officer had landed on a bag of papers that had cushioned his fall. I crouched beside him, the sweat from my face dropping onto his. I could tell he was beginning to come around.

My eyes moved down his body. The

name tag on his shirt read Shutt. His feet, covered in blood now, were still touching the last bag he had stabbed.

It looked as if the entire bed of the truck, once white, was now crimson.

"Look at me," I said when he first opened his eyes. "Shutt. Don't look down. Look right at me."

He immediately looked down and began backpedaling away from the blood, like a sand crab avoiding an approaching tide.

Blood splattered everywhere. On the bags. On him. On me.

And I wondered if the red rain falling on us might contain an infection, HIV or hepatitis B—something far more likely in here than on the street.

In his clumsy attempt to escape, the officer knocked me back into the bag with the body in it.

As I fell, it enveloped me, and I felt warm, sticky liquid on the back of my neck and soaking through my clothes.

Lurching forward, I pivoted slightly, a morbid part of me wanting to see. Lifeless black eyes staring blankly. Black head hanging unnaturally.

I slid forward trying to move away. When I sat up, I noticed that one of the nurses, a tall young woman with blond hair, had entered the sally port with us. Shutt was already off the truck moving frantically toward the gate where I had entered. The officer in the control room had the wits about her not to let him through.

I quickly jumped off the truck and had to hold onto its side as inside me all the blood seemed to drain from my head.

Within seconds, officers began pouring into the sally port from the other gates. Two immediately went over to check on Shutt. Another came to check on me. All of them straining to see into the back of the truck, which had taken on a surreal, slightly horrific quality.

"Chaplain, you okay?" Captain Skipper asked.

"Fine," I lied, nodding. "But let's get Shutt to Medical. He's really shaken up. And he's got blood all over him. We both need to get cleaned up."

"They're on the way," he said, and looked back at the truck. "Damnation. How can there be so much blood?"

"Heart must have still been pumping," I said. "How did everyone respond so fast?"

"Tower," he said as if it were obvious.

I looked fifty feet up at the tower to see the officer leaning out of the window observing everything below, radio still in her hand.

When I looked back down, I saw that the nurse had her arm around the distraught officer, talking to him reassuringly.

I walked over to them.

"Chaplain, can you help me for a minute?" the nurse asked.

A delicate, pale, blue-eyed beauty, she wore more makeup than she needed.

"Sure," I said, glancing at her name tag.

"Strickland," she said, trying but unable to remove the distressed look from her late-twenties face.

"John Jordan."

"I need to check on the inmate in the truck, John. Can you stay with him?"

"Sure," I said.

She turned to leave, but then turned back to Shutt and said, "I'm so sorry, but it's going to be okay. Everything's going to be okay."

She then ran over to the truck and bravely climbed onto the back.

Snapping on latex gloves, she carefully but quickly made her way to the bag with the body in it.

Crouching down to check the inmate, nearly disappearing behind the bags as she did, she moved with the surety and confidence of a seasoned ER nurse.

Moments later, the colonel and other medical personnel began to arrive.

Shutt and I were escorted out of the sally port and into the security building on the rear side of the control room.

It was difficult to see well from this new position, but I could tell that Captain Skipper had finished ripping open the bag to discover there was nothing left to do but call the coroner.

"I don't know if post-mortem prayers work, but if you have one, you might want to launch it up," Colonel Patterson said when he was buzzed into the hallway of the security building where we were standing.

He was a short, fat man with thick hands, bushy eyebrows, and messy hair. His uniform, which always looked sloppy, had large rings around the neck and armpits. His skin was leathery and his neck was red.

In my short time as a prison chaplain, I had met many decent, hardworking correctional officers. Colonel Patterson was not one of them.

"Why don't y'all come back to my office. We need to get your statements and have each of you fill out an incident report," he said as he continued to walk down the hallway toward his office.

The hallway, like all the hallways at PCI, was spotless and gleamed with the shine of a fresh coat of wax. Inmates had to have something to do.

In the colonel's office, we waited while he used the phone. His office was decorated with photographs, paintings, and trophies, all related to hunting. His desk was cluttered, a thin layer of dust covering it and everything on it.

The carpet needed vacuuming, and a distinct musty smell lingered in the air. Like the hallway, Colonel Patterson's office was included in the inmates' job assignment; but unlike the hallway, the room was not cleaned by them. They weren't allowed in here.

Paterson hated inmates and made no attempt to hide it. Rumor was, there had never been an inmate in his office. I believed it. There were other rumors about why the colonel hated inmates, many of which sounded like war stories, involving riots, gang attacks, and escape attempts, all starring the colonel himself. My theory was that the colonel just needed someone to hate, and since sixty-five percent of the inmate population was black, they made natural targets.

"I want the yard closed, the work crews recalled, and a count taken immediately," Patterson barked into his phone. "Call the superintendent, and ring him straight through to my office when you get him. Find Inspector Fortner, and get him back to my office with some incident reports."

If the colonel was upset by what had taken place, I couldn't tell. He always operated at fever pitch, always yelling orders, always coming on way too strong.

I glanced over at Shutt. He looked as if he'd just killed a man. His whole body, which appeared to be trapped in adolescence, trembled.

"You okay?" I asked him while the colonel reported to the superintendent what had happened.

He didn't look up, so I repeated the question. When he finally looked at me, he appeared to be in a trance, not knowing where he was.

"Huh?" he mumbled.

His pubescent face was a mask of shock and fear.

When he dropped his head again, I slid my chair over next to him. When I put my hand on his back, it actually shook from the force of the tremors running the length of his body.

"Colonel, Officer Shutt needs to see a doctor," I said.

"What? No he doesn't. Do you, son?"

Son didn't respond. He just continued to stare at the floor.

"Call Medical, now," I said, employing the colonel's method of communication.

"Ah, hellfire, Chaplain. He's been trained. He'll be all right."

"Call Medical now, or I will. And if I do, I'm going to declare a medical and psychological emergency. Then you can explain to them why you didn't."

The colonel snatched up the phone, pushed three buttons, and yelled into the receiver, "Get Medical to my office now." Hanging up the phone, he looked back at me. "Chaplain, you need to get a few things straight about the way things work around here. If I wasn't leaving this afternoon, I'd take you under my wing and make things real plain for you. But the short version is this: I—"

A quick knock on the door was followed by the entrance of the warden, Edward Stone, a deliberate-moving black man in an expensive suit.

"Colonel, Chaplain, Officer Shutt," he said by way of greeting. His eyes stopped on Shutt. "Have you called Medical, Colonel?"

"Yeah, they should be here any minute," he said curtly, as if he were talking to a new officer and not his boss.

"He's obviously in shock," Stone said. "How you holding up, Chaplain?"

I nodded. "Okay," I said, my voice quivering slightly with the anger I felt toward Patterson. "Just ready to get cleaned up."

"I heard how you responded to the, ah . . . situation very well. Control said you reacted with no hesitation. You never know until it comes down to it what a man will do in those kinds of situations. I know you're new, but everybody's trust for you just jumped up several notches. Isn't that right, Colonel?"

"Yeah, you never know what a man will do in a crunch," he said, careful to respond to Stone's first comment and not his second.

"Let's have Medical check out Officer Shutt and let the chaplain go home. We can take their statements tomorrow."

"Yeah, I think that's a good idea," Patterson said as if Stone had asked him.

Before anyone could say anything else, the colonel's phone rang and the medical personnel arrived to collect Shutt.

I helped him to his feet, assured him everything was going to be okay, and followed him and the nurses out of the office.

Just before I closed the door, I heard Patterson tell Stone that the deceased inmate in the trash bag was Ike Johnson.

I then walked over to the training building and took a long, hot shower and scrubbed his blood off my body.

2

I was half undressed when my doorbell rang.

I guess if I were more optimistic, I would say that I was half dressed—and that the glass of seltzer water without a coaster on my dresser was half full.

My dresser, like every other piece of furniture that I scrambled to get after the divorce, was not worth the trouble of a coaster. It had been a gift. Actually its previous owners did not know that it was a gift—all they knew was that they threw it out.

I was surprised when I heard the doorbell, not only because I was half undressed, but also because I had placed my order for pizza less than fifteen minutes before. It had always taken Sal's at least twenty-five minutes to deliver out here.

Since coming home to North Florida after my life in Atlanta had disintegrated, I'd made my home in a dilapidated old trailer on the edge of Potter County.

Quickly pulling my pants back up, I whisked by my gem of a dresser, pausing only long enough to secure the two folded bills on its corner.

The trailer had been repossessed, and its previous owners were obviously not a gentle breed. It was situated on a thatch grass prairie on what was supposed to be Phase II of an expanding mobile home community called the Prairie Palm. Presently, Phase II was a community of one, due in large part to Phase I, which resembled a trailer junkyard more than a place where people actually lived.

The park got its name from the lone sabal palm, Florida's state tree, standing in the center of the sixty-acre plot—something that seemed an appropriate metaphor for my isolated existence here.

As I walked down the extremely narrow

hall of my not-so-mobile home, passing over the pale yellow linoleum curling up so that it no longer reached the thin blond paneling of either wall, I remembered the plush two-story brick home Susan and I had shared in North Atlanta. It was nice. Very nice. But this impoverished place and the fringe existence I was now living here felt more like home.

I opened the door and extended the money in one flowing motion, more from practice than a God-given talent.

Expecting to see Ernie, Sal's nephew, who resembled the Sesame Street puppet of the same name, I made an audible gasp and suddenly felt naked without my shirt.

Instead of Ernie, I had opened the door to a young woman with big brown eyes in an orange, white, and blue uniform, which included a pair of tight-fitting navy blue shorts and a baseball cap.

She had shoulder-length brown hair pulled through the hole in the back of her cap to form a ponytail, and dark skin covering her taut, muscular little body.

She looked confused as I handed her the money, but took it reflexively.

I took the box from her and realized why she looked confused. It was a parcel not a pizza.

The oversized, blue block letters on its side read QVC, and then I remembered.

Last Friday night, while unable to sleep, I flipped past a shopping channel and did something I'd never done before. Made a purchase. This parcel contained my new IBM ThinkPad.

"No need for a tip," she said. "Just your signature."

"Sorry. Was expecting a pizza."

She handed me the plastic pen and electronic clipboard and flashed me a quick smile.

As I scrawled out my signature on the screen, I sensed her staring at the round pink scar on my left oblique and long, thin white scar across my chest.

When I looked up at her, she looked away.

"Pizza, huh?" she said, seemingly just wanting to say something.

In the distance, I could hear the sounds of poverty coming from Phase I of Prairie

Palm. People with time on their hands and not much else. Children yelling and laughing, the revving of automobile engines, and the loud, distorted music of cheap car stereos and boom boxes swirled together into the sad and badly mixed soundtrack of life in the rural South.

The only artist my ears could discern was John Mellencamp, which justified the volume. Appropriately enough, it was an acoustic version of his tribute to life in a small town.

I was born in a small town, and I live in a small town. Prob'ly die in a small town. Oh, those small communities.

"I'm sorry," I said. "I should have introduced myself. I'm John Jordan."

"Why?" she asked, her eyes narrowing.

Educated in a small town. Taught to fear Jesus in a small town.

Used to daydream in that small town. Another boring romantic, that's me.

"Why, what?" I asked.

"Why should you have introduced yourself? I'm just delivering a package. This isn't a social call."

"I . . . I thought you were having a hard time deciphering my signature."

"Your name is on the package," she said.

"Oh yeah," I said, shaking my head and frowning. "Sorry. I was just—"

"Relax. I'm sure a man in your profession introduces himself to nearly everyone he meets. Whether they want him to or not. What are you, a priest? Wait 'til I tell my friends I was hit on by a priest."

At first I couldn't figure out how she knew, but then realized my clerical collar was still hanging around my neck.

But I've seen it all in a small town. Had myself a ball in a small town. Married an L.A. doll and brought her to this small town. Now she's small town just like me.

"I'm the chaplain at PCI," I said touching my collar.

"I make deliveries out there sometimes. Big place."

No, I cannot forget where it is that I come from. I cannot forget the people who love me. Yeah, I can be myself here in this small town. And people let me be just what I want to be.

She turned to head back down the rocks

and pebbles and oyster shells that served as my driveway toward the big, colorful FedEx truck that matched her uniform, the blinking of its flashers rhythmic and hypnotic.

I was just about to ask for her name and maybe even her number when Ernie sped into the driveway, jumped out of his car, and ran to my doorstep, where I was still watching her.

Got nothing against a big town. Still hayseed enough to say look who's in the big town. But my bed is in a small town. Oh, and that's good enough for me.

"Sorry I'm late, JJ. Uncle Sal's getting slower and slower," Ernie said.

"You're not late. Just a little early."

He looked confused, then followed my gaze back down the driveway toward the truck she had disappeared into.

When I didn't take the pizza box he was trying to shove into my hands, he said, "You want the pizza or the pussy?"

"What?" I asked, digging into my pocket for the money with one hand and slapping him on top of the head with the other.

"I said that will be eight dollars and

eighty-nine cents," he said as he handed me the box.

I was still feeling around in my pockets for the money when I decided to take one more glance down the driveway.

She was standing in the opening on the passenger's side waving Ernie's money in the air.

"This one's on me, Preacher," she said. "I could use the tax deduction."

"Thanks," was all I could manage.

There was a time, not so long ago, when I'd've had a nice little buzz going by this time of the day and could've come up with a better response.

Ernie ran down the driveway to her truck and got the money faster than I would have thought possible.

They exchanged a few words, laughed, and then she drove off.

As Ernie ambled back, I walked down the driveway to meet him at his car.

Well I was born in a small town. And I can breathe in a small town. Gonna die in this small town. And that's prob'ly where they'll bury me.

"Please tell me you know who that was," I said.

"Sure, that's Laura Matthers. Her sister Kim and me are on the July jam court together Friday night."

"This Friday night, as in three days from now?"

"Uh huh. But she's got a boyfriend."

"Ernie, they almost always do."

3

The setting sun backlit the cypress trees, outlining them with a golden-orange glow as a gentle breeze rising from the surface of the river waved the Spanish moss draped over their twisted branches. Below, the wide Apalachicola River flowed inexorably towards the bay.

I was eating my pizza in an old, home-made wooden chair in my backyard partly because I found my single-wide trailer depressing—particularly when eating alone—but mostly because I found sunset along the banks of the river peaceful and calming, its flow spiritual in a way I couldn't fully explain.

The experience was restorative and the bloody events from earlier in the day receded some as if dimming into the soft-focus background of a photograph with a shallow depth of field.

I was about to take another sip of my Cherry Dr. Pepper when I heard a noise on the far side of my trailer and turned to see two kids, a boy and a girl, on bicycles bumping through the rutty grass toward me. The girl looked to be about twelve, the boy around seven, and I could tell from the condition of their clothes and the state of their bikes that poverty was their lot in this life.

I had seen them out riding their bikes in this mostly empty section of the Prairie Palm before, and figured they lived in the more populated Phase I.

Slowing, they hopped off their bikes and dropped them in the tall grass and continued toward me—all in one elegant and practiced motion that I suspected only partly had to do with their rickety hand-me-down rides not having kickstands.

"You Mr. Jordan?" the girl asked as they approached me.

She was a skinny preteen with long arms

and legs, straight blond hair past her shoulders, and blue eyes way too sad and wise for her age.

"I am," I said. "John."

"I'm Colby and this is my little brother Cody."

Both Colby and her little brother Cody were surreptitiously eyeing my pizza.

"How do you do?" I asked. "Would either of you care for a slice of Sal's famous?"

"I would," Cody said.

He was skinny and tall like his sister, but his skin was darker and his green eyes were smaller and more intense. Unlike his sister he was not wearing shoes, and he sniffled with a summer cold.

"*Co-dy*," she said, scoldingly stretching out his name.

"You're both welcome to some," I said. "There's far more than I can eat and I don't want to see it go to waste. You'd be doing me a favor. Please."

"Well, if it's just gonna go to waste . . ." she said.

"Y'all drag up a chair and help yourself."

Cody looked around. "Just you lives back here?"

"Just me," I said.

"We live over on the other side," Colby said. "With our . . . with the guy who was with our mom."

They dragged nearby homemade wooden chairs even nearer to mine but stood waiting for pizza without actually asking or reaching for it.

I handed Colby the box. "See if y'all can finish off the rest. I'm full."

She slowly took the box, then they both sat down a little cautiously and began to eat.

"This pizza is real good," Cody said.

"I'm glad you like it," I said. "Have you ever had Sal's before?"

"No, sir," he said as they both shook their heads.

They probably didn't eat out much—or ever—and given how hungry they were acting, I wondered if they eat in much either.

"Y'all ever eaten at Rudy's?" I asked.

"Yes, sir," Cody said.

"Once," Colby said. "Sort of. Our mom worked there for a little while when we first moved here. One time when Steve went to pick her up we rode with him and she let us sit at the counter and have a piece of pie each while she locked up."

"It was *good*," Cody said.

"She stopped working there 'cause Rudy didn't pay her what he promised," Colby said.

I nodded. "Think he's pretty bad about doing that," I said. "How'd you know who I was?"

"Heard some people talkin' about you," she said. "Looked you up at the library."

"Looked me up?"

"Yes, sir, I did. Old newspapers said you . . . that you used to be a cop . . . that you solved some crimes . . . Caught one of the Atlanta Child Murderers and . . . killed the Stone Cold Killer."

"Old newspapers said all that?"

When I was twelve years old and on vacation with my family in Atlanta, I encountered the Atlanta Child Murderer at the Omni Hotel. Six years later, I moved to Atlanta for college and to work the case. Eventually I became a member of the Stone Mountain Police Department and worked the Stone Cold Killer case too. And though I worked other cases, none had the notoriety nor left the scars those two did.

"Thing is . . ." she said, "our mom is missing and we want to hire you to find her."

"Will you?" Cody asked. "Will you help us find our mama, Mister? I'll mow your grass all summer. And she'll clean your trailer and cook for you. Please. We're good, hard workers."

4

Later that night I met Kimmy at the Sports Oasis.

Kimmy, sometimes Kim, Miller was a classmate of mine back in the day at Potter High School. She was petite and had a pretty, pale face, big brown eyes, and long, silky black hair she had taken to wearing in a ponytail since she became a deputy in my dad's department. She was smart and funny and attractive, but she was attracted to a certain type of emotionally unavailable men who the more they mistreated her, the greater her need for them grew.

The Sports Oasis was a second-story sports bar on Main Street in Pottersville that sat above a florist, a beauty shop, and an antique store. It was large and open and had the feel of a converted warehouse space. Between the long, curving bar on one wall and the stage on the other sat a dance floor and several high-top tables. Across the far wall were three pool tables and four dart machines.

Anna Rodden, the one that got away, was across the way with her husband Chris and I did my best to avoid looking at them and concentrate on the case, but it wasn't easy. I had waved to them from across the room when I first walked in, and planned for that to be my only interaction with them tonight.

Kimmy noticed me avoiding looking in their direction and said, "That's Anna, isn't it? Used to have a thing for her, didn't you?"

"Yeah," I said with a little smile. "*Used* to."

"Nothin' quite like the pull of the one who got away," she said. "I know all about that. And my conclusion on the matter is . . . unrequited love's a bitch."

I nodded and thought about how very right she was, even if mine wasn't exactly unrequited.

"Anyway . . ." she said, "maybe we should

go out sometime. We're both sort of single at the moment, aren't we?"

"Sort of," I said, "but it wouldn't be fair—knowing we're hung up on other people."

"Might not be fair," she said, "but it *would* be honest. Besides . . . who knows? We might just help each other get unhung."

"Well, since I know no one's ever gonna get you unhung from Ace," I said, "what can you tell me about the disappearance of Candace Miles?"

She looked at me for a long moment, her dark eyes locking onto mine, and started to say something but stopped, nodded and frowned to herself, and took another sip of her drink.

"I made a copy of the file for you," she said. "I hope I don't lose my job over it—I just got it. And your dad seems to like me—even mentioned making me the school resource officer. That's really what I'd like to do."

"Being at the school would put you in close proximity to Ace on a daily basis, wouldn't it?"

Ace Bowman, a coach at the high school, was the main emotionally unavailable man that Kim continued to go back to no matter how poorly he treated her.

"Not unlike working at the prison does you with Anna," she said. "Seems we both like our unrequited love with a side of masochism."

Unlike some of Kimmy's other men friends, Ace's mistreatment of her was largely of the indifference and neglectful and not the abusive variety, but I didn't want to think their dynamic was in any way similar to mine and Anna's.

"I thought that's the only way they served it," I said.

"Anyway . . ." she said, "Candace was a cocktail waitress here a few nights a week. She was pretty popular with the regulars. At least with the male-of-the-species regulars. She had, or has, big, beautiful, natural tits, and though she didn't exactly whore around, she did dress to . . . highlight the fact. She was attentive and flirtatious in the cocktail waitress sort of way, but from what everyone said, she went right up to the line but never crossed it."

"Interesting."

"How so?" she asked.

"Maybe an unstable regular was unsatisfied with that," I said. "His sick psyche felt humiliated or owed more than the tease, and he grew unhinged and acted."

"I wonder if the investigator asked around to see if someone was creeping her," she said.

"Whose case is it?"

"Cecil Dees," she said.

"Then probably not."

"If he weren't a fishing buddy of your dad's, no way he'd still be an investigator," she said. "And it's not that he's incapable of doing a good job, he's just too old and lazy. And I'd really, really just as soon that opinion not get back to your dad."

"None of this will get back to him," I said. "Remember, I'm the one who wanted to meet in secret. I could be asking him all of this."

"I meant to ask . . . Why didn't you want to talk to him about it?"

"It's complicated."

"I've been known to grasp a complicated concept or two in my time."

I smiled. "He's always pressuring me to come to work for him. Thinks I'm wasting my talents as a prison chaplain. Just didn't feel like getting into all that again right now."

She nodded. "I get it. Anyway . . . Candace's case is a bizarre one. She vanished after working a shift here on a pretty slow Sunday night two weeks ago. As it happens, I was here that night. Sometimes when I can't bear being alone in my empty house another minute, I come here. There were three people working here that night—Candace, Lina, and Kenny. All three are easy to talk to and I enjoy hanging out here with them —'specially on slow nights. Kenny, Lina, and I have the same taste in men. Oh, but don't say anything to Kenny about that. He's not all the way out yet. After their shift ended, the three of them sat for a minute and had a drink—a kind of ritual they have. When they asked her to have another, she said she had somewhere to be. She didn't say where, but didn't sound like to them that it was home with her boyfriend and kids. They finished so fast I was still in the parking lot by the time they came out. Lina doesn't have a car and had asked Candace if she could give her a ride that night, but Candace asked her if it was okay if Kenny did it since she was in such a hurry. The three of them pulled out of the parking lot around the same time—though in opposite directions. Kenny headed north toward Lina's place and Candace headed south, which wasn't in the direction of her place in the Prairie Palm, but none of us thought anything of it at the time. Unfortunately, I was headed in the same direction as Kenny and Lina. I wish had followed Candace instead. She pulled out first and we watched her drive away into the darkness. She was never seen again."

I looked over at Lina and Kenny behind the bar, but only for a moment since Anna and Chris were in my line of sight behind them.

"You remember that old wooden barn out on Highway 73 where they would sometimes slaughter cows and hogs?" she asked. "Near the McCall place. About to collapse at any moment."

"It's been about to collapse for twenty years," I said.

"True. Well, anyway, Monday morning her car was found abandoned there. It was at an odd, eerie angle, backed right into the side of the old barn. Unfortunately, the highway patrol officer who saw it and called it in just thought it was a drunk driver who walked away to keep from getting a DUI. He had it towed, essentially contaminating or losing all the forensic evidence it might have contained."

I nodded and thought about it.

"There are so many things off about this case," she said. "So many questions. So much suspicious behavior. And get this—the boyfriend never reported her missing. So when we sent an investigator out to their house to ask her about what happened, we thought we'd find her there hungover or something, but when Cecil started talking to Steve about it, that's the boyfriend, he said she never came home the previous night— something he only realized a little while before when he woke up. Said he fell asleep before it was time for her to be home. We found out later that their little girl, Colby, who is very mature for her age and takes care of the little brother, Cody, had gotten him ready for school and they had gone on their own."

"They're the reason I'm doing this. They

came over this evening and asked me to find their mom."

"Figures," she said. "We've got a couple of witnesses who saw the car not long after Candace left here that night. The three of them pulled out of here at a few minutes after eleven, and by quarter after, a man named Lance Stephenson passed by the old barn and saw the car backed into it. Said the headlights were still on and the left blinker. Said he turned around and drove back to check it out. Got out. Looked around. Said it was eerie as hell. Empty car idling in the dark night with no one around, lights on, blinker blinking. Said he looked all around and called out for the driver. No one ever responded. Never saw anybody or anything suspicious other than the car. Said he called the sheriff's department and reported it when he drove off, but there's no record of that call. A couple other passersby said they saw just the blinker and another said they saw just the headlights. No one ever saw Candice again."

"So whatever happened to her happened fast," I said.

"Exactly."

"Anything in her life now or in her back-ground that might—"

"From everything we could gather she seemed to be doing good now, but . . . she did have drug abuse in her background. Maybe even a little distributing—but only to support her habit. She got clean for her kids and it seems she stayed that way."

"What's the deal with her boyfriend?" I asked.

"He definitely raises some red flags," she said. "We've looked at him, but haven't come up with anything so far. Seems more of a deadbeat than anything else. Can't keep a job. Stays high or drunk most of the time. Blames the rest of the world for his failures. Two previous girlfriends filed domestic abuse charges on him but then recanted. One accused him of child sexual abuse but the investigation didn't turn up anything and the investigators concluded that it was just the girlfriend trying to get back at him for something."

"Was that lazy police work or actually the case?"

"Honestly don't know. Everything I'm telling you is what I've overheard from Cecil and your dad and others around the station and what's in the file. There's a lot I don't know. But there is one other thing that I do know. A couple of weeks before she disappeared, Candace was assaulted by a young woman named Mason Kelley. Do you know her?"

I shook my head. "If she grew up here I probably know her family, but I haven't been back long and her name isn't familiar."

"She's a piece of work. Always on something. Always looking for a fight. She was in here with her boyfriend—another real winner—and they were on more than alcohol, but they were on plenty of that, and Mason accused Candace of trying to steal her man. She actually said it like that. *Steal her man.*"

I laughed and said, "At some point did she start singing to her that she wasn't woman enough to do it?"

"Probably. Anyway . . . when Candace goes to get in her car after work that night, Mason jumps her and beats her up pretty bad. Two black eyes, cuts and scrapes on her face. Mason was charged with assault. She bragged to everyone who would listen that nothing would come of it, and since Candace has disappeared nothing has."

I glanced over toward Anna and Chris again to discover that sometime during our conversation they had gone, and I was grateful they hadn't stopped by our table on their way out.

"What's her boyfriend's name?" I asked.

"Steve," she said. "Steve Roberts."

"Mason's?"

"Oh. No. Sorry. That's Candace's. Mason's is named Kevin Turner."

"Okay," I said. "Thanks. And thanks for the file and all the great info. I really appreciate it."

"Do anything I can to help those kids get their mom back," she said. "And there's more to the story and my involvement, but I think I'll let Lina and Kenny explain that."

5

Half an hour after last call for alcohol, Kimmy and I were sitting with Lina and Kenny at a high-top table not far from where Anna and Chris had been.

"I still can't believe she's just . . . gone," Kenny said. "I mean, you hear about people vanishing without a trace, but . . . I don't know . . . I guess I always thought they were just being dramatic—you know, like on those true crime shows."

Kenny St. Johns was a tall, thin mid-twenties man with long, tapered fingers and very large feet.

"It still doesn't feel real," Lina added. "I

keep expecting her to walk through that door with one hell of a story, but the more time that passes..."

Lina Wilder was a late-thirties bottle-blonde with harsh features, darkish sun-damaged skin, and a low, raspy, whiskey-cured voice.

"The three of us," she continued, "weren't just coworkers but formed our own little island of misfit toys."

"I miss her every day," Kenny said. "Pick up the phone to call her several times. She was the kind of person you could tell anything. Always listened. Never judged. Ready with a hug or a kick in the seat of the pants."

Though barely perceptible, Kenny had the slight hint of a lisp, which became more noticeable the more he spoke, the more he drank, and the later it became.

"But as bad as I feel for whatever's befallen her," he said, "and how bad we miss her, it's her poor kids that most breaks my heart. And I'm genuinely worried for them."

"Me too," Lina said. "She was truly and totally scared—"

"Of Steve?" Kimmy asked.

"Yeah," she said.

"She was planning on leaving him," Kenny said. "And now he's got her kids."

"How do you know she was going to leave him?" I asked.

"'Cause we had promised to help her once she was ready," Lina said. "Hell, she and the kids were going to live with Kenny and his mom until she could get a place of her own."

"She had worked so hard to get off the shit," Kenny said, "and Steve, who was still on it, was always pressuring her to get high with him. And when she wouldn't . . . he'd get all aggressive with her, threaten the kids."

"Could he have found out she was planning to leave?" I asked.

"I don't know how," Lina said. "We were the only ones she told and neither of us breathed a word to anyone."

"Yeah, but . . . she was putting some money away, getting things ready in other ways," Kenny said. "Maybe he happened on some of that and found out that way."

"I would've sworn he did it, but they only had the one vehicle and they live way out in the Prairie Palm and he was with the kids that night. He couldn't've gotten to her to do something even if he wanted to."

"If it wasn't him," I said, "who else might it have been?"

"That bitch Mason," Lina said.

"Or her cute but assholey boyfriend, Kevin Turner," Kenny said.

Lina shook her head and contorted her face in disgust. "I fuckin' hate that guy. He's the worst."

"Anyone else?"

Lina said, "Candace is a looker, you know. Pretty face. Great smile. Smokin' hot body with tits for days. She was hit on—a lot. Could be some guy she rejected."

"There's a county full of them," Kenny said, "but . . . a few stick out." He looked around then leaned in and began whisper. "One is the owner of this particular establishment. He had her in a full-court press all the time and he's used to getting what he wants." He leaned back and raised his voice to a normal level again. "There was this dealer—used to be her dealer. Was always trying to give her product in exchange for sex."

"I think his real plan was to get her

hooked on it again and make her his sex slave," Lina said. "I've heard he's done it before. Gets a girl hooked. Uses her up. Then sells her to his customers."

"And then there's Creepy Carl," Kenny said. "One of our regulars we finally had to ban from the bar, he started harassing her so bad."

"But we always kept an eye out for her," Lina said. "There was nobody in the parking lot that night, and when she pulled out onto the road no one followed her."

"Okay," I said. "We'll follow up on all this. Thank you both. This has been extremely helpful."

"Oh, we're not done," Lina said.

"Our story is not over yet," Kenny added.

"It was something Candace said to me that night," Lina said. "She said no matter what happened or seemed to she was going to be all right, not to worry about her—that everything she was doing was for her kids, to give them a better life. I asked her what she meant, but that's all she would say. She just said that everything was about to work out for her, that she would be truly free and her kids would be safe. After Kenny dropped me off, I got in the shower like I always do and what she said just kept echoing in my head, you know? It was like . . . haunting me or something. When I got out of the shower, I told my roommate something was wrong. I started to call Candace, but since when she left she didn't head in the direction of home . . . I didn't want to call and just get Steve all riled up. So . . . I prayed about it . . . and I knew I had to do something. I called Kenny. Woke his mom up. Felt bad about that, but not too bad because I knew something was wrong. I told Kenny what I was feeling."

"I told her I was feeling the same thing," he said. "Women's intuition, girl."

It was the first overt reference to being gay he had made. Perhaps like his lisp, the more he drank and the later it got, the more open and out he became.

"Anyway," he continued, "a few minutes later I was back at her place picking her up. I called Kimmy since she had just been here with us and told her what was going on, and she met us at the bar."

"I had just laid down but I jumped right back up," Kimmy said. "On my way to meet them, I drove by Candace's place to see if she was home yet. She wasn't. Well, her car wasn't."

"From the bar," Lina said, "we headed in the direction she left. And just drove around looking for her."

Kenny nodded and said, "We drove past a few of her friends' places, one of her exes', and even her old dealer's. Didn't see her car anywhere. But here's the real kicker. We drove past that old falling down barn on 73 and I remember looking at it and wondering how it was still standing."

Kimmy said, "And this was well after Lance Stephenson and the other witnesses said they saw her car with the headlights and left blinker on backed into the side of the barn."

"And her car wasn't there," Kenny said. "No headlights. No blinker flashing. No car. No car at all."

"So," Kimmy said, "how could Lance and the others see it there before we passed by and the highway patrol find it there the next morning, but it wasn't there when we passed by?"

6

When I pulled out of the parking lot of the Sports Oasis, I turned north in the direction that Candace did the night she disappeared, following the route she had taken toward the old barn.

The night was dark and quiet, the rural road empty, the North Florida slash pines lining the road silent and still.

A sharp sliver of moon sliced a small tear in the fabric of the starless sky, while way down here below, the spill of my headlights caused shadows to dance in the ditches.

Thirty seconds from leaving the Oasis and I had already cleared the city limits, small town giving way to lonesome highway. Three minutes from leaving town and I was at the location where her car was discovered.

Beyond a leaning fence, its rotting wooden posts sheathed in briars and brambles and framed by oak trees, their thick, verdant branches hanging low and draped with Spanish moss, a small, overgrown livestock pen fronted an ancient, dilapidated pine-slatted barn with a rusted tin roof. Like the fence, the barn was covered in bushes and vines and was leaning to the left and tilted backward.

I parked on the side of the road and got out in the humid night, the sounds of cicadas flooding my ears.

Walking across the clay-covered culvert, I made my way toward the barn, tall, damp grass soaking my jeans.

Even now, twin trails of the tall Bahia grass were bent and broken from where Candace's car drove across the short, enclosed pasture.

When I reached the barn, I stopped and studied the place where her car had backed into the side of the barn, looking at the impact marks.

It was dark and hard to see much of anything, but being here gave me a real sense of
what it must have been like for her that
night, how alone and disoriented and frightened she must have felt.

*Who led you like a lamb to this place of
slaughter?*

*How'd he do it? With drugs? Threatening
your kids? Promising you the freedom you were
longing for?*

*Was this a prearranged meeting place or was
your crossing with the bad man a chance encounter?*

*Does this place have some significance for the
man who did this to you or was it just a place of
convenience?*

*Why here? Why was your car where it was?
Did he do that or did you? Were you trying to get
away?*

Walking back across the field to my car, I
wondered if Candace Miles was still here,
buried somewhere on the property with the
carcasses of cows and other once-living crea-
tures whose journeys stopped abruptly and
mercilessly here.

As I neared my car, a bright flashlight
beam blinded me.

"Put your hands up," a disembodied male voice in the darkness said.

I did.

"Who are you?" he asked. "What are you doing here?"

I told him.

"Jordan?" he said. "Any relation to the sheriff?"

"He's my dad."

"You got ID on you?"

"I do," I said. "But I'm not about to reach into my pocket until you turn that light on yourself and show me you're not pointing a weapon at me."

He turned the light on himself to show me his hands and I very slowly and carefully withdrew my wallet and showed him my driver's license.

He was a young man with a military haircut and bearing, and a uniform that looked as if he just took it off the ironing board where he used extra spray starch on it.

He told me who he was as he studied my license—he was the highway patrol officer who'd found Candace's car and called it in. He had just been passing by and saw me out here and wondered if I might not be Candace's killer returning to the scene.

"You think she's dead?" I asked.

"Huh?" he said, handing my license back to me.

"You said you thought I might be the killer returning to the scene."

"Oh," he said. "I guess I do. If you could've seen the way that car was smashed into that barn . . . it took a brutal, violent force. Liked to have never gotten it out. Hadn't really thought about it but I guess that's why I think she's dead—that and it's going on three weeks that she's been gone."

I nodded and frowned. "Hope you're wrong but I'm afraid you're right."

"It's partly my fault," he said. "I should've never had the car towed before letting forensics process it. No telling what all evidence was lost."

"If y'all had every car left on the side of the road processed by a crime scene unit, that's all y'all and they would be doing."

"Yeah, but . . . this one was different. The way I found it. I should've known. I should've . . . I just screwed up."

I didn't say anything.

"Was hoping you were the killer and I was going to get to redeem myself," he said. "Can't image how excited I got when I saw you."

"Sorry," I said.

"That you're *not* the killer?"

"Well, no, not exactly that."

"Tell you what," he said. "You can make it up to me by finding her. Preferably alive."

7

The following morning I stood at my desk in my chapel office inside Potter Correctional Institution, a stack of mail and the package containing my new computer in front of me.

Moving the unopened mail to one side, I ripped into the box and extracted the computer inside, releasing a flurry of small packing peanuts as I did.

At that moment, Warden Stone walked in without knocking.

Every muscle in my body grew tense.

"Chaplain, I need to speak with you for a moment," he said as he closed my office door behind him.

He made no attempt to hide his annoyance at the floating Styrofoam swirling around him as he removed two handfuls of packing peanuts from the chair across from my desk before sitting in it.

Stone was always dressed impeccably in expensive suits that looked to be tailored, and he always took great care to protect them. Had he been aware of the sweaty, soiled inmate uniforms that normally occupied the seat, he probably would have left the peanuts in place.

As I sat down, an envelope on top of my lopsided stack of mail slid off, revealing an inmate request form from Ike Johnson.

Stunned, I quickly opened my center drawer and placed it inside.

Before he started talking, Edward not Ed Stone paused to clean his charcoal wire-rimmed glasses. Like everything he owned, they looked expensive. As he removed them carefully from his face and wiped them with the spotless white silk handkerchief bearing his initials in bold black block letters, he treated them like they were costly jewels.

As I watched him, I realized that the

glasses, like everything he owned, seemed so expensive because he treated them that way.

As he made these exact, intentional motions, I had a chance to really look at him for the first time. He was much leaner than I had thought. I had seen skin that was darker than his, but not by much. He had all the African features of a man from Nigeria. His nearly hairless skin was smooth and had a slight sheen about it. His movements were slow but not hesitant—more deliberate and economic than anything else. He knew exactly what he was doing and the precise amount of energy required to do it. He did everything as if it were the most important thing he would do that day.

Edward Stone's minimalist actions and conservative, controlling policies reminded me of the effects poverty and fear and fear of poverty have on people. No matter how successful they become, they always keep plenty in reserve for fear they will have to do without again. My grandmother, a child during the Great Depression, had been the same way.

"How are you?" he asked. "With what happened yesterday?"

I nodded. "I'm fine. Thank you."

"That was bad. Have to be an idiot to try to escape, but to try it in that manner . . . you'd have to be suicidal."

"Perhaps he was," I said.

"Maybe. I don't know. But that's what I want to find out. The thing is, his name came up in another matter that we're considering investigating."

"Really?"

"Yes. I had not put much stock in the earlier reports, but now . . . I am not so sure. Thing is . . . we have a situation that I need your help with."

I waited.

"It won't be easy . . . and it's totally out of the purview of your job. But I honestly do not have anyone else I can turn to."

I nodded encouragingly.

"I want you to help the IG with the investigation into . . . what happened yesterday."

I started to object, but he stopped me with a single authoritative wave of his hand.

"I conducted a thorough background check on you long before I ever decided to approach you with this, and I know that you and the IG don't care for each other very much, but there's no other way."

"Even if you could convince me to work with him, you'll never get him to work with me."

"I've already taken care of that through the secretary."

"His *secretary*?"

"No. *The* secretary of the department," he said with an amused smile. "So, like you, he really doesn't have a choice in this matter."

"But—"

"Your father being the sheriff here doesn't hurt, but even if he weren't, you're . . . exactly who I need to . . . take care of this. I know you used to be a cop. Know you worked the Atlanta Child Murders. I know you've studied criminology. It's even rumored you were the one who killed the Stone Cold Killer."

"As impressive as that is," I said, trying to sound only mildly sarcastic, "wouldn't the institutional inspector be a better choice?"

"To be completely honest, I don't trust Pete Fortner. Ordinarily, I would have the colonel assist in this kind of investigation, but he'll be away from the institution in training for the next few weeks."

"Why don't you trust Fortner?" I asked.

"First of all, I need to know that you'll do it."

I thought about it. I had been trying to leave the obsession and violence and negative energy of homicide investigations behind me, but I could feel the strong pull of what was being offered to me. It was seductive.

"I'm a chaplain now," I said. "That comes first. But if I can do both, I am willing. I will. But I will not work closely with the IG. Because *I* don't trust him."

"Okay, the reason I'm asking you is because Daniels is Fortner's boss. Fortner's looking for a promotion, and he'd sacrifice my institution to get it. I don't trust the two men together. You, on the other hand, Daniels hates. You're the best man for the job."

At that moment, my phone rang.

"Good morning. Chaplain Jordan," I said into the receiver.

"Chaplain, this is Officer Jones in the

control room. Is the warden in your office by chance?"

No, not by chance. He leaves nothing to chance.

I handed Stone the phone. He took it without comment or expression.

"Stone . . . Yes . . . okay, send him over to the chapel right away."

He handed me the receiver and I hung it up.

"Your new partner has arrived. Before he gets here, I just want to make clear your responsibilities. You are to assist him in the investigation in any way that you can, but I also want you looking out for the institution and its administration—and report to me every step of the way."

The front door to the chapel opened and the warden stood to open my office door for the inspector.

I remained seated.

When the inspector walked in, he and Stone introduced themselves to each other.

Tom Daniels was fifty-five, but looked sixty-five. His battleship-gray eyes matched his hair, which still showed no sign of receding.

When they had finished shaking hands, Stone sat down again, pulling his pants legs up slightly and crossing his legs. He then steepled his hands together in front of his face as if praying, the tips of his fingers at his lips.

Daniels just sort of collapsed into his chair.

Tom Daniels had the look of an alcoholic. I knew, being an alumnus myself. His face was red and swollen, his nose pink and puffy, spiderwebbed with little blue broken veins.

Though an obvious alcoholic, he was a high-functioning one. He worked hard. Presented well. Yet he was often late, and didn't produce the results he once had. And though he made a good salary and lived modestly, he was plagued by financial problems.

He was dressed in gray slacks that matched his hair and eyes, a white shirt that matched his pale skin, and a red tie that matched his bloodshot eyes.

The effect of alcoholism on Tom Daniels was severe, but its effects on his family were devastating. Though never beaten nor abused, his wife and daughter had been neglected.

His daughter, though a teetotaler, functioned as a dry drunk and an enabler. She lacked confidence and any idea how to relate to men in general, and a husband in particular. She attracted, and was only attracted to, alcoholics. I knew. I had married her.

"I believe you know our chaplain, John Jordan," Stone said.

"Yeah, I know him," Daniels said without as much as a glance in my direction.

"As I am sure you're already aware, he will be assisting you. He grew up here and knows many of the employees of the institution."

I had been away for so long, it felt like I didn't know nearly as many people as I used to, and many of those employed by the prison commuted from other communities.

"I've been told I don't have a say in the matter," Daniels said irritably.

"So has he," Stone said.

Daniels cut his cold, dull eyes in my direction and smirked. "What about the institutional inspector?"

"He'll help too, but you are to limit his knowledge and access."

"You better have a damn good reason for that," Daniels said.

"I do."

When he didn't explain, Daniels said, "Oh yeah? What's that?"

"A good reason."

"No. I mean what's the reason?"

Stone smiled. "You have copies of all the files and reports that I have. You know as much about it as I do. So I'm going to let you brief Chaplain Jordan. At the end of the day, report back to me. Both of you."

Stone then stood and left without another word.

"Before we even begin this little exercise in futility," Daniels began, "I want to get a few things straight. I don't like you. I've never seen a more hypocritical sight in all my life than you in a clerical collar, 'cept maybe it makes you look like the little candy-ass faggot you really are. This is my investigation and you better stay the hell out of my way. I'll be watching you—waiting for you to fuck up. When you do, and I know you will, I will personally bury your ass. Deep."

8

Dostoevsky said the degree of civilization in a society can be judged by entering its prisons.

I often thought about that as I entered PCI each day.

At times I believed the condition of our prisons spoke well of our civilization. In some ways, we as a country take great care of those we incarcerate—of course whether most of them should be incarcerated in the first place is another matter.

The fact that convicted felons don't lose their freedom of religion. The fact that I was employed by the state to ensure the guarantee of that right. The fact that I was here to counsel inmates and help them deal with crises—both inside prison and back at home. All spoke well of our approach to imprisonment.

Other times I was disheartened by the inhumanity and incivility that I witnessed.

There's no question that mass incarceration, particularly as it affects African-American men and other impoverished minorities, is out of control in our culture. The prison industrial complex largely runs on the injustice of our justice system. Yet once we take custody of inmates, we by and large take care of them.

Of course there is abuse. Of course there is neglect. But from what I witnessed on a daily basis, these are largely isolated incidences, the abuses of power by isolated individuals rather than a systemic problem within our prison system.

One of the ways we care for the incarcerated is by the way we classify each according to his crime and custody level, his skills and abilities, and his psychological and medical needs.

In a prison like PCI, there are all types of inmates—those who received a DUI and resisted arrest, those who sexually abused children, those who committed murder, rape, or theft—the last usually in the pursuit of drugs. There are inmates who are dangerous and others who are themselves in danger. Putting all these various individuals in one institution is a very precarious endeavor.

Some inmates are violent. Others are not. Some are escape risks. Some you'd have a hard time getting to leave. Others need close medical or psychological supervision. And all must be assigned a job that they are qualified to do, even if it's just picking up trash.

The department responsible for giving inmates a security evaluation and a job assignment, as well as determining whether or not they are a risk or at risk, is Classification.

Since Daniels made it clear he didn't want me working with him, and because the feeling was mutual, I decided to conduct a little inquiry of my own, beginning with a classification officer named Anna Rodden.

Anna, who I had been in love with since childhood, was my older sister Nancy's best friend all through school.

"Anna," I said after tapping on her door.

She was seated behind her desk wearing

a sleeveless white silk blouse and a fire engine–red skirt, with the matching jacket draped over the back of her chair. Her long brown hair was gathered in a single long ponytail at the nape of her neck, held by a red and white bow. The white of her shirt made her olive skin look even darker. She was dark in other ways too. As she looked up from her work, I was again amazed at the depth of her seemingly bottomless brown eyes.

"John," she said, sounding happy to see me.

I loved the way she said my name.

"Come in," she continued. "How are you? I heard what happened yesterday. I was just about to call you."

"I'm okay."

"You sure?"

I nodded. "How're you?"

"Had better days. Escape attempts are difficult enough, but when the inmate gets killed..."

"Was he one of yours?" I asked.

She nodded. "Everyone from Central Office on down wants to know why I didn't know he was an escape risk."

I nodded and frowned.

Had I taken this job in part so I could see her every day? Would I continue to do it once she left?

She was in the final stages of finishing her law degree at Florida State, and would soon be one of the state's toughest prosecutors.

"What brings you my way today?" she said.

"Stone has asked me to look into what happened yesterday."

Before I had finished my sentence, she was shaking her head.

"That's the one thing I won't help you with. I can't."

She had witnessed firsthand the darkness and violence my relentless and obsessive investigative techniques had brought into my life.

"I know you haven't forgotten what Atlanta was like," she added. "So you must just be blocking it out. But I can't."

I understood and appreciated her concern, but things were different now. *I* was different. I was older. I wasn't drinking. I wasn't in a bad relationship.

I had moved to Atlanta in 1986 to work the Atlanta Child Murders. I had only been eighteen at the time. Most of the work I had done on that case and the Stone Cold Killer case that followed was in my early twenties. It was now 1995. I was twenty-seven years old, far, far better equipped to deal not just with homicide investigations but life itself. Or so I believed.

"This is nothing," I said. "A simple—"

She let out a harsh laugh. "Nothing is ever simple with you, John."

"I really think this can be. I'm just taking a quick look into it. I thought with you and Merrill here to keep me honest I'd—"

A quick knock at her door stopped me.

It was Tom Daniels.

"Yes?" she said as he stuck his head in the door.

"My name is Inspector Daniels."

"Your mother named you Inspector?" she said. "Sort of limited your career options, didn't it?"

"Cute," he said. "I think you know. I'm the Inspector General of the DOC."

"What can I do for you, Inspector General?"

"It's a private matter. Can I talk to you alone?"

She shook her head.

"Fine," he said. "We can do this in front of—"

When he came around and saw it was me, he shook his head and said, "Should've known."

"Are you following me?" I said.

Ignoring me, he dropped into the seat next to mine.

"I'm looking into the death of the inmate yesterday," he said to Anna. "Ike Johnson. Is he yours?"

"Is he my what?"

"Is he your . . . Was he assigned to you? Are you his classification officer?"

"I was."

"What can you tell me about him?"

She shook her head. "Not much. Before yesterday I would've sworn he wasn't an escape risk. Could be something new going on with him I don't know about yet. You should probably ask his pimp."

"Who's that? The chaplain?"

She frowned. "So childish."

"And what were you being earlier?" he

asked. "All I need is a little information. Why're you being so damn difficult? Who's his pimp?"

"Inmate named Jacobson."

"What's Jacobson like?"

"Pretends to be crazy—which he is, but not in the way he pretends to be. He acts looney but he's truly dangerous."

"Okay. Thanks. I'll talk to him. What about Johnson's family situation on the outside? Who'd he have?"

"Grandmother who raised him and an aunt that I know of."

"No girlfriend?"

"He didn't like girls, never has."

"Faggot on the outside, not just in here?"

"Use language like that again and you won't get any more information from me. I don't care who you are."

"Sorry. I just . . . Didn't mean to give offense. Sorry. What I meant was . . . Was he a homosexual for real and not just for convenience the way some of 'em are in here?"

"Ike was gay. If you're asking if I am aware of a lover he would have tried to escape for, I am not. He did have four visits from a Don Hall when he first got here, but that was over a year ago."

He jotted something down in a small notebook and said, "Anything else?"

"I've just started looking," she said. "I . . . Like I said, I didn't think he was an escape risk. Obviously I missed something."

He stood, withdrew a card from his pocket, and placed it on the desk in front of her.

"This is an official investigation of a death within this prison. A death in which you are at least partly to blame. Call me the moment you come up with anything else. Don't tell the chaplain or anyone else. Only me. No matter what it is. Understand?"

She nodded without saying anything.

"And don't discuss my case or anything about it with anyone but me. Not the chaplain. Not your mama. No one."

Without waiting for her to respond, he turned and walked out of the office, closing the door a little harder than was necessary—but not hard enough to be overly obvious.

She shook her head and narrowed her eyes at me. "Know how to pick 'em, don't you?"

"Whatta—"

"That was your ex-father-in-law, wasn't it?" she said.

I frowned and nodded.

"I never liked Susan," she said. "Now I know why. What an ass. You two are working on the same case?"

"We're supposed to be working it together."

"You don't seem too together."

I smiled. "That's about as together as we're ever gonna get."

"I've changed my mind about helping you with the case. Hell, I'm gonna help you solve it before that smug, obnoxious ass does. But I'm gonna be keepin' a close eye on you. If it gets too—"

"It won't."

"So how can I help?"

"Do you know for a fact that Jacobson was Johnson's pimp?"

"As much as you can know such things for facts inside here. They were both assigned to me."

"What was his job assignment?"

"Not pimp, I can tell you that."

"I meant Ike Johnson."

"Outside grounds," she said, seeming not to catch how odd that was.

Inmates who worked outside of the institution did so because they were deemed to be a low escape risk. It had to do with their custody, their release date, and past history.

"Outside the gate?" I asked. "You sure?"

She nods. "I know."

"He works outside the gate five days a week, but he tries to escape in the trash truck on his day off?"

The vast majority of escapes occurred while an inmate was already outside the prison—work assignment, court hearing, transport, medical procedure. Breaking out of a maximum-security prison was extremely difficult to do—nearly impossible.

"What else can you tell me about him?" I asked.

"As you can imagine, he spent a lot of time in Confinement for physical contact with other inmates. And sometimes drug use."

"By *physical* you mean sexual contact, right?"

"Sure wasn't for fighting. You see how small he was?"

He had fit in a garbage bag but before this moment I hadn't realized how small that meant he had to be.

"Skinny too," she added. "He had HIV and AIDS."

I thought about being covered in his blood.

She must have seen something in my eyes.

"You came in contact with his blood, didn't you?"

"Contact is one word for it. Swimming. Drowning. Are a couple of others."

"The chances that you could be . . . are so small . . . Are you worried?"

"Didn't even know to be until a minute ago."

"Don't be. Get tested. Just for peace of mind. But don't worry. I'm sure you're absolutely fine."

I nodded. "Okay. I'm not really worried," I lied.

"Good. Because you're fine. But if you get worried and need to talk . . ."

We were quiet a moment and I thought about what happened yesterday in light of what I now knew about Johnson.

"If he really wanted to escape . . ." I said, thinking out loud. "He'd've tried it while outside for his job, right? He sat there in that bag and heard what the officer was doing to all the other bags. He knew what was coming."

"You're thinking suicide?" she said.

"Considering the possibility. But there are much better ways to commit suicide. Maybe it was murder."

"*Murder*?" she said.

"Everybody here knows how the garbage is checked before it leaves the front gate. It'd be a great way to hide a murder or have one committed."

"So somebody kills him and puts him in the garbage bag so he'd be dumped somewhere or get stabbed and it would look like he was trying to escape."

"I think if it were an escape attempt, he'd've lost his nerve there at the end. And maybe even if it were suicide."

"Maybe the officer had been paid to miss that bag," she said.

"That's good. But if he was, that meant he knew the inmate was in there, which meant he knew he was killing him. Which means he deserves an Oscar for the performance he gave. Hard to fake shock like that. What can you tell me about Jacobson?"

"He was in the infirmary with Johnson on Monday night."

"What?"

"Yeah. And they had a fight. Tuesday morning Jacobson was taken to Confinement and locked up, and Johnson . . . Well, you know what happened to him."

"What time was he placed in the box?"

"Log indicates it was around six thirty in the morning. Of course, those logs are never exact."

"No, but it's probably close to the actual time, which means he could have killed him and bagged him before he was taken away."

"Maybe. I don't know. Seems to me that whoever did the deed would have to actually load the bag on the truck. Otherwise . . . it'd be too heavy . . . obvious a body was inside, wouldn't it?"

"It may not mean anything, but then again . . . He was locked up before the shift change. And yet, it was close to the time of the shift change. Too close."

"Whatta you mean?" she asked.

"From what I've seen, if something occurs that close to the shift change, the officers leaving save it for the officers just coming in."

"That's true," she said. "They definitely do."

9

Potter Correctional Institution was its own little world—a society of captives and captors with its own social order, classes, economy, and laws.

Neither captive nor captor, I wasn't just an outsider, I was a stranger in limbo between the two groups.

I needed a guide into the first group, and the first and most obvious choice was the inmate assigned to the chapel to assist me, Mr. Smith.

I was told during orientation not to call any inmate *mister* or *sir*, but I made an exception for Mr. Smith.

Mr. Smith was an old black man whose

back was slightly bent, causing him to bow forward a little as he walked.

Life had bent but not broken this man.

As he walked, with his head down, a small bald spot could be seen right at the crown of his head. He was raised in the old Southern school of repression, in an era when a black man was to be seen and not heard—seen working, that is.

Mr. Smith and I had developed a good rapport since I had been at PCI. After returning from Anna's office, I decided to ask him to explain a few things to me about life on the inside, but when I reached my office there were several inmates waiting to see me.

On an average day, I had contact with over a hundred inmates, twenty of whom usually came to my office for some form of crisis counseling.

Some inmates actually came to my office out of a desire for rehabilitation, recovery, and spiritual growth. Most came over trivial matters relating to their jobs or bed assignments or wanting to use my phone.

"Chap, I's wondering if I could use your phone," Inmate Jones, an elderly, slow-talking, and slow-moving black man said when we were seated in my office. "My aunt is real sick. I need to call my peoples."

"I'm sorry," I said. "As you know, the department will only allow me to place a phone call for you in the event of the death or serious illness of an immediate family member. Even then I have to verify it by an outside official like a doctor or funeral director."

"Just this once. I really need to talk to her. She raise me, you know."

"Is she at home or in the hospital?"

"She at home."

"The only thing I can do is give you a phone pass that will allow you to call from your dorm. I'm sorry."

I opened my desk drawer to retrieve a phone pass form. As I did, I saw the inmate request from Ike Johnson. In my discomfort and distress of dealing with Daniels I had forgotten about it. I quickly closed the drawer.

"She got a block on her phone," he said.

If he perceived the contradiction in what he was asking for with what he was saying, he gave no indication.

If she really wanted to hear from him,

why would she have a block on her line? I often wondered how inmates could tell me with a straight face how close they were with their families and yet admit that their families had gone to the trouble of placing a block on their phones that prevented them from calling.

"If she has a block on her phone, she obviously doesn't want to be called. Have you tried writing her?"

He stood up angrily and stormed out.

As soon as he was gone, I opened my desk drawer again and pulled out Ike Johnson's request.

The triplicate inmate request forms are how inmates ask for help from staff members in prison.

From Ike Johnson to Chaplain Jordan. *Dear Chaplin sir, I really need to talk to you very soon. Can I come to your office tomorrow? It's real important. I'm scared I'm either going to try to escape or kill myself and don't know who to talk to. Sir, you my only hope. May God bless you, Chaplin sir.*

Unlike any other request I had ever received, this one was typed. Most inmates didn't have access to typewriters, and the ones who did were only allowed to use them for official reasons such as legal work.

I glanced up at the date. It was dated the day he was killed. I should have received the request yesterday, but his death and my involvement in it had delayed me getting it.

I reread the request several times.

The type had several distinguishing marks. The letter *t* was missing the right side of the crossbar, the letter *o* was missing the bottom curve, and the letter *a* was much darker than the rest of the type. The typewriter that produced this request shouldn't be difficult to find.

While I was examining the request, Mr. Smith tapped on the door.

"Come in," I said.

"Brother Chaplain suh, they's two more to see you now."

Mr. Smith's blue uniform was always neatly pressed and buttoned all the way to the top.

"Do you know what they want?" I asked.

"One say he didn't get the Father's Day card we sent him. The other one wants you to make copies of his legal papers."

"Sounds like things that can wait a few

minutes. Come in and sit down and let's talk for a minute."

He slowly swaggered in and took his seat. "I done something wrong, suh?" he asked.

"Not at all. I need your help."

"Okay suh. Do what I can."

He was slumped so far down in his chair as to be nearly horizontal, his head hanging to the side as if too heavy to hold upright, and his long arms dangling on either side of the chair.

"I'm still trying to understand how things work on the compound and wondered if you could explain a few things to me."

"Like what?" he asked, caution and suspicion creeping into his voice and body language.

"How often do you hear inmates talking seriously about trying to escape?"

"Not many ever say anything like that to me. Too hard. Chances are they couldn't make it. Not worth it. This place harder to get out of than it look."

"Anyone ever escaped from here before?" I asked.

He had been here almost the entire three years this institution had been open.

"No suh. Not as I know of. Couple from the work camp did, but they caught them lickety-split."

"Any thoughts about what happened yesterday?"

"Nigga a fool. Everybody know what they do to them bags. Must have wanted to die."

"So you don't think it was a serious escape attempt?"

He shook his head. "No suh. Either he want to die or somebody want him dead."

"What's the drug and alcohol situation on the compound?"

"They's those who have it. They's those that would love to have it but can't afford it. They's those who do anything for it."

"Lot of it on the compound?"

"No suh, not a lot. But more than you'd think. Homemade hooch, buck, pills, grass, coke, meth."

"How does it get in?"

"Most the liquor is homemade. Inmates in Food Services or the chapel sneak juice or old fruit and sugar back down on the 'pound. Mix it up. Let it ferment."

"You mean inmates have stolen our communion juice to make buck?"

"Oh, yes suh. Some go to church on communion night just 'cause of it. They hold it in they mouth, spit it in a pill bottle or bag they stole until they get back down to the dorm, and empty it into an old can or plastic bag. Clerk worked here before me used to steal it. Sell it down on the 'pound."

"What about the drugs?"

"Come in during visitation or staff bring it in. Some inmate family member sneak it in and slip it to them while they visit, or leave it in the bathroom and the orderly get it when he clean up. They also officers, staff what bring it in to sell."

"Is it expensive? Hard to get?" I asked.

He nods. "Sex, cookies, cards, smokes, favors—beat up or kill someone for it."

"No cash involved?"

"Most everything done on trade. Inmate say, 'You do this for me or that for me and I give you my canteen.' They pay—it just ain't with money. If money involved it happen on the outside. Inmate family or friend pay a staff member out there to bring somethin' in here."

"What about sex?" I asked. "I heard Ike Johnson was a workin' girl."

He nods. "It just like on the street. They's punks, pimps, sisters, and the gay and straight inmates what use they services. Punks are the real gays. They gay before they come in here. Some have pimps what look after them, hire them out. Sisters are only into each other. They got no protection, don't hire out. They just in love, I reckon."

We were both silent a moment.

"You said some straight inmates use the services of some of the prostitutes," I said.

He nods. "They straight on the outside. Just can't get none in here. So they have to . . . make do. But they only pitch. Never catch. In here they a big difference between pitchin' and catchin'."

We were silent again, and I mused about the equivocations of pitching and catching in the social order of Potter Correctional Institution.

"Some of the punks wears women's stuff," he said.

"Like what?" I asked.

"Panties, pantyhose, perfume. Shit like that."

"Where do they get it?"

"Buy it off female officers. Even trade

some of them sex for it. Funny, ain't it? Gay guy givin' sex to womens in exchange for girly stuff for they man."

It was certainly among the more ironic things I had encountered in here.

"Thing you gots to remember about this place. If an inmate do somethin', most of the time it because officer or staff allow him to."

"Most of the inmates trust you, don't they?" I said.

"I got respect. Not the same thing. Most inmates don't trust no one. They life say they can't trust no one, not even the chaplain. You gots mine. Probably get a few others. Not many."

"If an inmate wanted to escape, could an officer be bought to help?"

"Probably not. They sell you dope, maybe turn they head when you beat up a punk, but they wouldn't help you get out. Too risky."

"How well did you know Ike Johnson?"

"Not really at all."

"What about Jacobson?"

"Yeah, I know him. Watch your back 'round him. Some people say he crazy, but he ain't. He dangerous. Lot of inmates say they kill before. Most of 'em ain't. But Jacobson for real."

"I appreciate you talkin' to me," I said.

"Someone else you should talk to," he said. "Old homosexual on the 'pound. Say very little, but he know a lot."

"What's his name?"

"Don't know his real name. Everybody just call him Grandma."

10

I ke Johnson had spent the last night of his life in the infirmary. Jacobson had been there too.

The medical building, like every other building at PCI, was gray cinderblock with light blue trim. It housed Dental and Classification also, and its waiting room was always filled with inmates.

When I entered the small, crowded, but quiet waiting room, I was presented with a choice. The locked door to the left led to Classification and Psychology, the locked door to the right, to Medical, Dental, and Pharmaceutical. I chose right—away from Anna, whom I would rather be visiting again—and as I unlocked the medical department door with my key, I wondered how many other staff members carried a similar key. It made sense that a chaplain would. I spent a great deal of time in the infirmary. But who else had one? Who else had access to the victim the night before he died?

Walking down the long hallway toward the infirmary, I passed the nurses' station where two nurses sat—one white, one black, both elderly and overweight. Each had an inmate seated across from her and was laboring to check his vital signs.

I also passed by two exam rooms. In one, Dr. Mulid Akbar, PCI's senior health officer and one of the chapel's advisors on the Muslim religion, was examining the knee of one of the inmates, who seemed to be in a great deal of pain.

At the end of the hallway and to the left, I entered the officers' station for the infirmary. There I found, to both my surprise and delight, the nurse who had helped during the incident in the sally port the previous day. She was seated on the officer's desk, swinging her legs back and forth and chewing gum while conversing playfully with an officer named Straub.

She smiled when she saw me.

I smiled back.

"Hey, Chaplain," she said. "Jordan, isn't it?"

"John, please, but yes. How're you?"

"Better than the last time I saw you," she said. "How are you?"

I nodded. "The same."

"That was . . . brutal. I . . . I didn't sleep a wink last night. You?"

"No, but I usually don't."

"By the way, my name is Sandra, but everyone calls me Sandy. Sandy Strickland. I don't think we've met yet. Not really."

"John Jordan," I said. "Nice to meet you Sandy."

"You too—I can't call you John. Will have to be Chaplain."

"Please call me John."

"I'll try, but no promises."

"Never seen you here during the day before and now two days in a row," I said. "You been transferred to day shift?"

"Oh, no. I'm too much of a night owl. I wouldn't be much use around here most mornings. Getting ready for an ACA inspection. Tryin' to get everything ready. Plus with what happened yesterday . . . here to help if I'm needed."

"We keep trying to get her to join us on day shift," Officer Straub said, never taking his eyes off her.

Ignoring his obvious flirtations, she said, "I keep thinkin' about what happened yesterday . . . It was just so . . . horrible. So much blood . . . everywhere. It really got to me. Think I'm gonna step outside a minute for some fresh air. You wanna join me, Chaplain?"

"Sure."

The fresh air was far too hot and humid to be refreshing, but it did seem to do Sandy some good. Of course it could've been the super slim Capri cigarette she was inhaling.

We were standing at the back right corner of the medical building. It was a popular designated smoking area, but for now we had it all to ourselves.

"You okay?" I asked.

She nodded. "Mostly needed a break from Straub."

"Did you know him well?" I asked.

She looked confused. "Who? Straub?"

"Johnson."

"Oh," she said, shrugging. "Some. About as well as you can know any of the inmates, I guess."

"He in the infirmary a lot?"

"More than most, but . . . not a ton."

"Anything you can tell me about him that might help me understand what happened?"

She shook her head. "Not really. Nothing that would explain—"

"How about just anything about him."

"He was kind of small. Slightly effeminate. Got bullied. And worse, I think." I nodded. "I heard he had a pimp."

"Really, who?"

"Jacobson."

She nodded. "He's been in to see us a few times. I try to avoid him. He's . . . unbalanced. So he was . . . That really pisses me off. The shit this place does to people. A little sweet guy like Ike. Wish I'd've known. Jacobson. Sick of . . . Tell you what, if you're not a criminal when you get here, you'll damn sure be one when you leave."

Her eyes glistened, and I was touched by her compassionate anger.

We were silent for a moment, Sandy enjoying her cigarette, me enjoying the day.

"Wait," she said. "They were together in the infirmary the night before . . . Ike was killed."

"Anything happen between them? How did Jacobson wind up in Confinement and Johnson . . . in the back of that truck?"

She shook her head and shrugged as she gazed into the distance. "I really don't know. It was a relatively quiet night. They were the only two we had in the infirmary that night. In the early morning hours of Tuesday—five maybe—they started yelling at each other, and before too long Jacobson was on top of Johnson punching him in the face. The officer on duty, Officer Hardy, wasn't at his desk, so Captain Skipper and I broke them up and separated them. He told them to go back to bed and he would forget about it. I've never seen Skipper do anything like that before. Told them if they did it again, he was going to write them a disciplinary report and send them to Confinement."

"Where was Officer Hardy?" I asked.

She shook her head and gave me a frustrated expression. "I have no idea where he goes. He wasn't where he was supposed to be."

"What days does he work?" I asked.

"Hardy? Thursday through Monday, but Monday night was his last night for two weeks. He's on annual leave now. Pretty convenient, huh?"

"Why was Captain Skipper down here that night?"

"I think he came to take a statement from one of the inmates involved in an incident earlier that night, but he wasn't here."

"Which inmate?"

"Thomas, I believe."

"Anthony Thomas?"

"Yeah. You know him?"

"I've worked with him some. Where was he?"

"No idea. But he's in Confinement now. Skipper locked him up for not being where he was supposed to be."

"How long did Skipper stay?" I asked.

"Not long at all," she said. "Left when he couldn't find Thomas."

"What happened next?"

"Not sure. They must've started fighting again. Officer Hardy had Jacobson locked up.

Strange he didn't have them both locked up. I went back up to my desk to finish some paperwork, and that was the last I saw either of them. Until . . . the truck."

"Who else was in the building at that time?"

"Let's see. Nurse Anderson, and our inmate orderly, Allen Jones. I believe he was gathering the trash and cleaning the exam rooms."

"What about the trash? When is it picked up?"

"Early in the morning usually. I'm not really sure. Our orderly always gets it ready and puts it out here to be picked up."

"Is that orderly here now?" I asked.

"Yeah, I think so," she said.

"Mind if I speak to him?" I asked.

"Not at all. Let's go see if we can find him."

She took one last, long draw on the stub of her cigarette and tossed it into the ashtray.

We found her orderly, the same old black man I had denied a phone call earlier this morning, in one of the storage closets near the back. She told him I wanted to talk to him and that we could use the staff break room around the corner.

I could tell he didn't want to, but he swaggered toward the break room nonetheless.

"This won't take long," I said when we were finally seated at one of the tables in the staff lounge.

He didn't respond.

"Sorry again I couldn't let you use my phone this morning."

He shrugged.

"I just want to know how you normally gather and take out the trash down here and if you did it any differently on Monday night or Tuesday morning."

"I gather it up before I leaves every night and puts it near the back door where you's just standing with Nurse Strickland. Next mornin' I picks up any new trash and sets them outside the door. Officer and inmate from inside grounds comes by and picks it up and takes it out."

"Is that how it happened Tuesday morning?" I asked.

He shook his head slowly. "Already told

the inspector. Gathered it all up and put the bag in the back hall, then Nurse Anderson come say she need me to clean up a spill in the exam room. When I come back to put it outside, it was done gone. Nurse Anderson with me at the time. She can tell you. Trash wasn't outside the door neither. No sign of the truck neither."

"Did you see the inmates in the infirmary that morning?" I asked.

He nodded.

"Anything unusual about them?"

"No, sir. All three were lying there in they beds sleepin'."

"All *three*?" I asked, the surprise in my voice obvious. "Who else was there?"

He hesitated and looked confused. "Johnson, Jacobson, and Thomas."

"What time were you in there?"

"Can't say for sure. Gots no watch. I come in at four. Wasn't too long after that."

"You see Jacobson and Johnson fighting around five?"

He shook his head. "I's still gathering up the trash and cleaning up. I's all over the building."

I walked back to the nurses' station and

called the trash officer, who I had been in the back of the truck with yesterday.

"Officer Shutt?"

"Yeah."

"It's Chaplain Jordan. Just wanted to see how you're feeling."

"Better," he said. "A lot better. Thanks. And thanks for your help yesterday. I just freaked."

"I understand," I said. "I'm surprised you're back at work so soon."

"Just trying to stay busy," he said, sounding a little defensive. "Tryin' not to think about it. That's all. Wasn't . . . It was just an awful accident."

"I just keep wondering how he got into that trash bag in the first place," I said, trying to make it sound like an idle curiosity.

"That's a good question. I wonder that too. I usually pick up the trash from every department early in the morning. They set it outside their back door, and me and an in-mate pick it up. But yesterday, there was no trash outside of Medical."

"Really?"

"Yeah. I parked between Medical and Laundry like I always do. I usually stay in the truck, but I had to ask the laundry sergeant about an inmate who used to work for him, so I walked over with the inmate. When we came back with the bags from Laundry, Medical's were already gone. They must've put them in themselves."

"They ever done that before?" I asked.

"Sure, but not very often. And usually we see that old black inmate 'cause he's so slow, but we didn't see anybody. Why all the questions?"

"I'm just trying to figure out exactly what happened."

"I'll tell you what happened. A dumb inmate tried to escape and became a dark meat shish kebab. Everybody's saying what a great thing I did. Hell, I'll probably get Officer of the Month. And if anybody has anything else to say about it, they can say it to my lawyer."

"Your *lawyer*?" I asked.

"Hell, yes," he said. "I been grieved and sued so many damn times by these dumb sons a bitches I had to get one. What kind of world do we live in? A bunch of stinkin' inmates can make me need a lawyer."

11

Every eleven minutes, someone in the US died of AIDS.

In Florida state prisons, those with HIV outnumbered those in Florida's free population two to one.

Many inmates came into the system infected with HIV—primarily the result of shared needles and unprotected sex.

In the close confinement of prison it spread rapidly.

Tattooing, drug use, unprotected sex caused HIV to spread inside prison the way the virus was designed to.

Only six state prison systems in the US

distributed condoms. Florida wasn't one of them.

With these thoughts bouncing around my head, I had gone in search of Sandy Strickland. I found her in an exam room inventorying supplies.

"You got another minute for me?" I asked Sandy Strickland.

"Of course," she said as she turned around to face me, her blue eyes sparkling even under the dull fluorescent lights. "Come in."

When I closed the door behind me, she looked a little surprised.

"What is it? You okay?"

I sensed genuine concern. She was a good nurse. I had come to the right place.

"I . . . wondered if you . . . might . . . This is harder than I thought it'd be."

"Take your time. It's okay. Whatever it is . . . we'll . . . figure it out."

"I found out today that the inmate who was killed yesterday, the one whose blood I was covered in, had AIDS."

She nodded slowly.

"I can't quit thinking about it. Can't . . .

concentrate . . . Just keep thinkin' I might have been infected."

"Oh, you poor man," she said. "I know exactly how you feel. Blood is such a scary thing these days. I come in contact with bad blood all the time. It scares the hell out of me too."

"Should I be scared?" I asked.

"Unless it penetrated your skin or splashed into your eyes or mouth . . . even then you'd—"

"The officer freaking out splashed it everywhere."

"I can test you. Give you peace of mind. But I wouldn't worry. Chances are good you weren't infected."

I nodded. "Thank you. It helps just talking about it."

"I can test you privately down here. Nobody else has to know."

"Thank you. Thank you so much."

She motioned for me to sit on the exam table.

As she worked around me, I thought how ironic it was that I might be infected. Not only had I been in a married monogamous relationship until recently, but I was extremely careful inside here every day.

When she was finally ready to draw my blood, she put her delicate hands on me, patting, squeezing, caressing, comforting. She even held my hand as she withdrew the blood.

"How long does it take?" I asked as she busied herself labeling the vial of blood and disposing of the needle.

"We'll have to do a series of tests. This first one will be back in about a week, give or take. I'll sneak it in with some other tests. I'll call you the minute I know. And then we'll do another test in a few weeks, and another in about three months just to be absolutely certain."

"You're an excellent nurse," I said. "How did you wind up here?"

"You mean in prison?" she said with a smile. "Old sour Sister Mary Margaret said I'd wind up in prison one day. I worked for a doctor in Tallahassee . . . and . . . we got involved . . . needed to get away."

"Tallahassee's loss is our gain."

"Didn't mean to get into all that, but . . .

you're easy to talk to. Maybe we can do more of it outside of this place—over coffee or something."

12

"Were dogs used to search the area around the barn for Candace?" I asked.

With one of the few free moments of my day, I sat down at my desk and called Kimmy to ask her more about Candace's case.

"Yeah," she said. "Search dogs—prison's K-9 unit—not cadaver dogs. Do you think we need cadaver dogs too . . . ? Because that's way above my pay grade. You'll have to talk to your dad about that."

"Did the search dogs turn up anything?"

"Alerted on the car, of course," she said, "then tracked a path around it, hit on a place on the ground where they think she may have fallen down or been put down for a while. I hate to even say it but . . . if she was raped it could've been there, or if she was killed it could've been where her body was laid before it was moved. Then they continued to a place back toward the road and that's where the scent ended."

I thought about what that might mean.

"So," she said, "whether he killed or abducted her . . . it's probably where her body went into another vehicle."

"Or," I said, "if she staged all this or was involved in it in some way, it could just be where she walked over and got into another vehicle on her own."

"Oh," she said. "Wow. Hadn't really considered that. So . . . how do we find out? What's next?"

"There are some things that need to be done," I said, "that will require . . . that are of an official nature, and I really don't want to do anything official. Are you willing to do that part?"

"Sure," she said. "As long as Cecil or your dad don't find out. I'm just a lowly deputy— and a girl to boot. I can't be caught doing man's work—*particularly detective man's work*."

"We'll make sure you don't get caught," I said. "Do you know who owns the land the car was found on?"

"Yeah, a man from Alabama. He inherited it. Says he hasn't been down here in years. Just keeps paying the property tax on it because it meant so much to his dad and granddad. Cecil said he took a look at him and there just wasn't anything there."

"Do you know or have y'all looked at who lives on the backside of the property or across the street or anywhere around it? I think it'd be worth finding out, just in case he used it because it was familiar to him or close to where he lives. Most criminals stick to what's familiar."

"I'll find out."

"Cool. And I really think we need to take a look at Steve's and Candace's phone records—see who they've been talking to. Do you know if Cecil got those? They weren't in the file, so I'm guessing he didn't."

"I don't think so."

"Can you figure out a way to get them without anybody knowing?" I asked.

"No," she said, "not really."

"Okay," I said. "I'll give that one some thought."

"Oh, but I did just find out something very, *very* interesting," she said.

"Oh yeah?"

"Remember me telling you about that Mason Kelley chick who attacked Candace in the parking lot of the bar for trying to steal her loser boyfriend, Kevin Turner?"

"Yeah."

"Well, guess what? Though a good bit younger than her, Kevin is one of Candace's exes."

"Really?"

"And rumor has it he may actually be her son's biological father."

13

There are four types of lockup in the Florida state prison system.

Protective-management lockup is for those who are at risk in the general prison population—rapists, child-molesters, ex-law-enforcement officers.

Close-management dorms are for those who, because of their custody, crimes, and behavior on the inside, are confined to a cell.

Confinement has two classifications—administrative and disciplinary. An inmate is placed in administrative confinement when the administration determines that it is best to do so—usually when he is under investigation for a crime. Disciplinary confinement is for those inmates who were accused of a crime and were found guilty. Jacobson was in the latter.

Whereas most inmates in the Florida DOC are housed in open-bay military bar-racks–style dormitories, those in lockup are housed in single six-by-nine cells. Some of the lockup cells house two inmates, some one. All have a sink, toilet, two bunks, and a very small window covered with steel mesh.

Inmates in lockup are fed through a slot in the metal door about the size of a food tray. Jacobson's was open, and I was talking to him through it.

Squatting down to talk through the tray slot in the door always made my knees ache and my feet fall asleep. I usually chose to talk to an inmate through the tray slot because of the security hassle involved in arranging to meet him in his cell or the conference room.

For me to enter an inmate's cell, he must be frisked and cuffed, and an officer must be present at all times. The same is involved if I meet with him in the conference room.

Many times what the inmate has to say to me is so short that being frisked and cuffed takes longer than our meeting. Other times the inmate has a lot to say, but is unable or unwilling to because of the security officer standing within hearing distance.

I was hoping that without an officer present, Jacobson would talk openly.

"Fuck you, motherfucker," he said.

Guess open communication wasn't going to be a problem.

From the last cell down the corridor to my right, I could hear the inmate Starn yelling, "CHAPLAIN, CHAPLAIN, COME HERE. COME HERE, CHAPLAIN."

He did that every time I came to Confinement. It was Wednesday, and I had already seen him twice this week.

Crouching down on the bare cement floor, I smelled the same odor I always did—sleep.

The stale air was thick.

Drool. Perspiration. Halitosis.

Behind me, the gray block wall was lined with empty milk cartons, wads of crumpled napkins, and various other items of trash the inmates had tossed out of their cells.

Jacobson's cell was one of twenty along a long corridor. An officer, a round, bald-headed black man, was seated at the end of the hall. Another officer, a tall slender man with strawberry blond hair and pink cheeks, was crouched down by a food slot about five cells down from me.

"Nothing I can help you with?" I asked. "Nothing you'd like to talk about?"

"I said, fuck you motherfucker."

From the next cell an inmate yelled, "MOTHERFUCKER DON'T TALK TO THE CHAPLAIN LIKE THAT. YOU *STUPID* SON OF A BITCH AIN'T YOU GOT NO RESPECT."

Deciding to change my approach, I said, "From what I hear, you would, but I'm not interested."

"Ain't no punk," he said.

He may or may not have been a punk, but what he looked like was a neo-Nazi serial killer. Shaved head. Pale white skin. Sparse beard. Prison-green tattoos. Shark eyes.

"What are you then?" I asked.

"I'm Satan, man," he hissed.

"Don't be so hard on yourself," I said.

"Shee-it, don't be so hard on Satan," the inmate to my left said, and started laughing.

"You come to cast me out, Holy Man?" Jacobson asked.

"Actually, I just wanted to see if there was anything I could do for you and maybe ask you a few questions."

Somewhere in another corridor a steel door slammed. The noise bounced off the concrete walls and floors and reverberated through Confinement.

"We're locked in now, boys," another inmate said.

"Nothin' you could do for me," Jacobson said. "I'm well taken care of. What you really mean is, there's something I can do for you. You need something I have."

"CHAPLAIN, CHAPLAIN," Starn continued to call.

"Which is what?" I asked.

"Secrets."

The officers' radios sounded at the same time, and because of their distance apart and the cement surroundings, every word was doubled.

"What makes you think I want to know your secrets?" I said.

"I see evil. I hear evil. I speak evil."

"What sort of things?" I asked.

"I've crossed my heart, hoped to die. Watch it, or I'll stick a needle in your eye. I'll cast *you* out, Holy Man. I can have you stuck, just like Johnson. Was it in his eye? COs are so sloppy. I heard it was messy. Did all his blood drain out? There's power in the blood. Life and death. Atonement's in the blood. But I guess you know that. You think he atoned for his sins?"

"CHAPLAIN, CHAPLAIN. CHAPLAIN, I NEED YOU," Starn yelled.

"You had Johnson stuck? What was his sin?" I asked.

"I can have anybody I want to stuck," he said.

As he talked he widened and narrowed his eyes.

"But I like sticking pigs best," he added. "Hickory, dickory, dock—Johnson didn't have a cock, but he got one . . . every night, and now he's taken flight."

"CHAPLAIN, CHAPLAIN," Starn yelled, his voice sounding sad and whiny.

"Did you have Johnson stuck?"

"The pig had him stuck because he was tired of getting stuck in the butt."

He jumped up suddenly from his crouched position at the slot and began dancing around the cell, crashing into the sink, bed, and walls as he did.

Then he started singing. *"There is power, power, wonder-working power in the blood of the lamb."*

"Jacobson," I said. "Jacobson."

"Power, power, wonder-working power in the blood of the lamb."

Evidently the officer at the nearby cell heard me, and rushed over and looked through the narrow glass window of the cell door. He yelled for the other officer, who was still seated at the end of the hall, to come quickly and began to fumble for his keys.

"CHAPLAIN, CHAPLAIN."

"Step back, Father, please," he said.

His voice was an octave higher from the excitement, his fine strawberry blond hair moving about as he moved, and his face, previously pink, was now deep red.

I complied.

He pulled the handcuffs from the back of his belt and opened them. As soon as the rotund black officer joined him, Strawberry Blond unlocked the door and stepped in, Rotund following closely behind him. As Rotund entered the cell, I could have sworn I saw him smile.

"Would you be free from the burden of sin? There's power in the blood, power in the blood."

Strawberry Blond told Jacobson to assume the position.

Jacobson responded with many colorful obscenities, some of which I had never heard before.

Suddenly Jacobson was on the floor.

It happened so quickly it took me a moment to realize that it had.

While Strawberry Blond was telling Jacobson to turn around and spread his legs, Rotund stepped up and punched him hard at the base of the neck.

In a matter of moments Jacobson was cuffed, face down on the rough concrete floor, then snatched up to his feet, a mild abrasion now on his forehead.

"Let's get him to Medical," Rotund said. "See about these cuts." Then he added to Jacobson, "Next time I'm using the gas."

"You better ask your captain first," Jacobson whispered.

"Nobody touch this blood," Rotund said

as if he hadn't heard Jacobson. "It's bad blood in more ways than one."

"Let me call the OIC first," Strawberry Blond said, beginning to walk back toward his desk. "Chaplain, can I talk with you for minute?"

"Sure," I said looking back at Jacobson, who stared blankly at the wall in front of him.

As we walked down to the officer's desk at the end of the corridor, I learned that Strawberry's name was Rogers. When we passed by Starn's cell, I stopped and looked in.

"Chaplain," Starn asked, "do you believe that a demon can possess a man?"

"We already talked about this, Starn," I said.

"I'm scared," he said in the small voice of a scared child. "Satan wants me."

"Nothing spiritual, good or bad, can happen to you that you don't allow," I said. "I'll come back and talk to you again in a few minutes. Okay?"

"Okay," he said in an upbeat voice, soothed like a child.

When Rogers and I reached his desk, he sat down.

I stood across from him.

"What happened to make him go off like that?" he asked.

"I really couldn't say. He was okay, and then all of a sudden he exploded. Does he often do that?"

"He does pretty much whatever he wants around here," he said.

"Whatta you mean?"

He frowned. "Certain inmates are looked out for around here."

"Who gives that kind of preferential treatment to an inmate as unstable as he is?"

"He's not unstable. He's a damn actor. Did you say anything about Johnson to him?"

I nodded. "Why?"

"That's the only thing he seems to genuinely get upset about. I think he's scared for real about that."

"Do you think he had anything to do with it?"

"He had everything to do with Johnson. They were both down here constantly. So either he had something to do with it or it scared him shitless, excuse my language, because he didn't."

"Like if he didn't do it, it was done in part as a message to him?" I asked.

"Think about how it was done," he said. "It was a message to someone."

I nodded. "No doubt."

Rotund yelled from down the hall, "Come on. What's taking so long?"

"Just a minute," Rogers yelled back.

I glanced at my watch. It was almost time for my meeting with Tom Daniels and Edward Stone.

"What's gonna happen to Jacobson?"

"He'll be taken to Medical, checked out, and probably taken to the isolation cell and sedated and watched for twenty-four hours. That is, unless Captain Skipper cuts him out. Then he could be sent back down here or who knows? There's no telling. Hell, I just work here."

"What's the difference in being confined in one cell as opposed to another?"

"Not much during the day, but I've heard at night all sorts of weird shit happens in here."

14

They looked like men sitting around a barber shop on Saturday morning. Nowhere to go. Nowhere they had to be. Nothing but time to kill. Inmates don't have much, but what they have—time —they have a lot of.

They sat around the chapel library under the watchful eye of the officer temporarily assigned to watch them until my new assistant, a Jewish chaplain, was hired next month. Mr. Smith and three other inmates were reading *Decision* magazine, the monthly magazine that the Billy Graham Evangelistic Association faithfully sent us free of charge. Mr. Smith and one of the other inmates were wearing headphones—listening to gospel music or a recorded sermon.

On my way to meet with the warden and the IG, I decided to stop by the chapel to check in on things.

When Mr. Smith saw me, he jumped up and walked out into the hallway where I was unlocking my office door. "They's two what want to see you, Chaplain."

"Okay," I said, "but it will have to be when I get back. I've got a meeting with the warden in about ten minutes."

"I tell 'em to wait. So hot out there, they won't mind. 'Sides they gots nothin' else to do."

"Thank you," I said, and walked into my office.

As I closed the door, the phone began to ring.

"Chaplain Jordan," I said into the receiver.

"This the chaplain?" a distressed female voice asked.

"It is," I said. "How can I help you?"

"This is Veronica Simpson. My husband Charles Simpson is an inmate there. I need to talk to him. I haven't heard from him in four months, and I need to talk to him right now. I'm not playing with you, and I'm not crazy, but I've got a gun to my head, and I'm going to use it on myself and his two-year-old son if I can't talk to him right now."

"Okay," I said, "now listen to me. I will let you talk to your husband, so just put the gun down and relax."

"I'm not crazy. I swear," she added quickly, her voice seeming to gain strength. "If I can just talk to him, I won't kill myself."

"The thing is, he is not here right now," I said, talking very slowly. "It will take a few minutes, but I will have him called up right away. So, why don't we talk until he gets here? Would that be okay?"

"That would be okay," she said softly. She was beginning to sound calmer.

"I have to ask you to hold on a minute while I call down to his dorm and have him sent up here. Is that okay?"

"That's okay. I'm not going anywhere. I'm all right, Preacher. I just want to talk to my husband. I won't do anything foolish. Promise. Just as long as I can talk to him."

As quickly as I could, I pressed hold, then the second line, and punched in the number to the control room. Without going into much detail, I told the sergeant in the control room to find Simpson and get him to my office as soon as humanly possible.

I then punched line one again, hoping she'd still be there.

She was.

We talked about five minutes, waiting for her husband to come to my office. Our conversation dealt primarily with all the pressures she faced being a single mom whose husband was incarcerated.

I actually felt as if I did her some good, but chances were I'd never know.

When Simpson finally did arrive, after what seemed like days, I quickly put him on the phone and went into the other office where I called the Tampa Police and reported her threat of suicide. While talking to her I had discovered where she lived, and I told them. I then jotted down a few notes about what had transpired and called the OIC and filled him in. He advised me to fill out an incident report, which I did. I then walked back into my office and sat down at my desk.

Noticing that Simpson was crying, I

busied myself with opening the rest of my mail.

My mail consisted of roughly fifteen requests from inmates for everything from Bibles and greeting cards to phone calls. There were also two letters from citizen volunteers who ministered at the prison saying what a blessing they themselves were, a memo from the chaplaincy administrator about upcoming religious holidays that were to be observed by the Jewish, Muslim, and Christian inmates, and a single piece of typing paper trifolded and taped together on the end with the word *Chaplain* typed on the outside.

I unfolded the typing paper, tearing it slightly while removing the tape. It read, *I've seen you talking to her. I watch over her. If you don't stay away from her, I will kill you like I did that little bastard yesterday. She's an angel, and I'm her guardian. She's mine. Stay away from her.*

I reached into my desk and pulled out the request from Ike Johnson. I laid them both on the desk in front of me and began to compare them. Within seconds, I could tell they were typed on the same machine.

I thought of Anna as I reread the note.

"I'm sorry, what'd you say?" I said when I realized Simpson was talking to me.

"Thank you, Chaplain. I thinks she going to be all right. I should have called her or written or something. It's my fault, but this place is getting to me. I don't know what to do."

"Why don't you start coming to see me every week for a while, and you might want to think about seeing the psych specialist as well."

"Okay," he said. "I will."

"And, stay in touch with your wife. It's tough in here, but it's tough for her out there too."

"I know. I will. Thank you."

15

The warden's office was neat, orderly, and as conservative as he was, with one exception. In the center of his wall of fame, amid the diplomas, merit certificates, and department commendations, was a hand-drawn picture of a family—a husband, a wife, and a child. The artist used crayons and showed great potential—potential he never got to live up to because of his untimely death at eight years old.

Edward Stone and his wife never tried for children again after that.

"You're late," Stone said.

"Sorry."

"Let's get to it. Don't have much time left. But first, shut the door."

I did. Then took the chair next to Daniels.

"Inspector, what do we have so far?" Stone asked.

"In some ways, a great deal of information," he said, sitting up and leaning forward slightly. "But in other ways, not very much at all. I am finding your people very uncooperative."

Daniels looked as if a day's work felt like a week's. His shirt ballooned out just over his belt, the way you would expect it to if it had been worn all day without a retuck. His face was red. And large, conspicuous drops of sweat trickled down the sides of his cheeks.

"Surely the chaplain has been helpful with this," Stone said.

Unlike Daniels, Stone looked as if he had just finished getting dressed—morning fresh and military crisp.

Daniels began to speak, but I jumped in. "As soon as you left us this morning, the inspector expressed his desire to work alone and left."

"Inspector?" Stone said.

"I've made it clear from the very beginning that I won't work with him," Daniels said, the sweat on his forehead increasing. "I am fully capable of conducting this investigation on my own. I certainly don't need someone like him botching up my case."

"If, as you say, you are fully capable of conducting this investigation on your own, how is it that you are having difficulty doing so?" Stone asked.

"I'm not having difficulty investigating. I am having difficulty with these mother-loving rednecks around here. I have gathered a lot of information about the inmate who was killed, though."

Daniels withdrew a wrinkled, soiled handkerchief from his back left pants pocket and wiped his forehead. It merely smeared the sweat around. It also left some lint on his eyebrow.

"But you will work together, or I will call the secretary. Understood?"

Daniels didn't respond.

"Understood?" Stone said again.

Daniels made a slight nod with his head.

"Understood?" Stone repeated, looking at me.

Nodding, I said, "I understood it the first time."

"Now, tell me what you have, Inspector," Stone said.

"I can tell you that Johnson was murdered," Daniels said with a swell of pride that changed his posture. "The inmate was unconscious before he was ever placed in the bag. ME says he was full of enough chloral hydrate to be dead soon anyway."

"What is chloral hydrate?" Stone asked.

"Sleeping pills."

"Couldn't he have taken them himself?" Stone said. "Maybe to relax during his escape or because he wanted to die?"

"I don't think so. I think he was drugged by someone who knew that putting him in the trash bag would get him stabbed to death."

"Did the ME say how the drug was administered?" I asked.

Medical personnel might use a syringe. An officer might put it in food. Another inmate might give it to him as a pill or powder and tell him it's some other kind of drug.

Daniels's face turned even redder. It was obvious he hadn't asked.

"He was unable to say conclusively," he said. "We should know shortly."

"What else do you have?" Stone asked.

"He had an abnormal number of lacerations, even for an inmate. A few abrasions that were not related to his death."

"Where did the fatal blow strike him?" Stone asked.

"Bottom part of his heart. The rod got stuck in his rib cage. Shutt broke several ribs trying to get it free. But that's not what killed him."

"What?" Stone asked.

"ME says that the rod scraped the bottom of the heart, but really didn't pierce it. The loss of blood would have killed him eventually. He lost a shitload of it in a hurry, but it still takes a while. He didn't die immediately. Died as the result of a blow to the throat that dislocated his windpipe."

"Could the officer have done that or even known what he was doing?" Stone asked.

"Maybe. I don't know. Your prime witness is sitting right across from you. Why don't you ask him?"

"I'll get to him in a minute," Stone said

with a quick glance in my direction. "What else can you tell us?"

"He was a drug user. There were traces of crack and alcohol in his blood."

"*Crack*?" Stone said.

Dust was visible in the shaft of sunlight shining in through the window, specks dancing in it. Amazingly, it seemed to avoid Stone.

"So his death could be drug-related," Daniels said.

"Aren't drug screenings done periodically?" I said.

"Yes, they are. He was tested as recently as a week ago, and it was negative. Besides, he was in Confinement most of the time, which makes it virtually impossible to get drugs—or anything else, for that matter."

"That's not what I've heard," I said.

"What have you heard?" Stone asked.

"That some strange things go on around here at night. Especially in Confinement."

Neither man reacted or commented, and Daniels continued.

"He was a . . . gay. Had AIDS. There were traces of semen around his . . . on him. It is being processed at FDLE. Maybe we'll get lucky and get something from it. Who knows?"

"How about you, Chaplain?" Stone asked. "You discovered anything useful?"

"I have more," Daniels said.

"Let's have it."

"The lab also found some unusual trace evidence—a PRIDE chemical on his blues. May give us an idea of where he was before he wound up in the trash heap."

PRIDE is a state-authorized not-for-profit company that operates inside Florida state prisons, training inmates for general manu-facturing and services. Many of the products created by PRIDE are used inside the prison.

"Chaplain? What about being our prime witness? Can you tell us anything else about the actual stabbing yesterday?"

"I really don't think I can add anything to what I've already said."

"Should Shutt be looked into?" he asked.

I nodded.

"Okay," he said, and then he looked at Daniels again. "Have you ever heard the old saying, 'You can catch more flies with honey than vinegar'?"

"Sure, I've heard it," he said.

"Well, the chaplain here is your honey. He is well liked and respected, and he knows at least half of the staff pretty well. So, you are to work with him and not without him or you are not to work in this institution at all. Understand?"

"Yeah, I understand."

"Understand, Chaplain?" Stone said to me.

"Yes, sir."

"Good. Now go find out what's going on in my institution."

16

"There are a lot of things I regret," Steve Roberts, Candace's live-in boyfriend was saying.

His maudlin disposition matched the liquor on his breath.

We were sitting in a pair of rickety lawn chairs in the mostly dirt yard in front of his trailer, as Colby and Cody rode their bikes around the narrow streets of the subdivision.

"Do you have regrets?" he asked.

He was wearing a frayed wife beater, khaki cargo shorts a few sizes too big for his emaciated frame, and thin, green dollar-store flip-flops. He had a bottle of Beam in one hand and a glass he kept refilling in the other.

"Many," I said.

"What do you do?"

"Live with them," I said. "And sometimes what you're doing."

"Huh?" he asked. "What I'm doing?"

"Trying to drown them."

"I guess I am. I just . . . I feel so . . . I miss her so much. Don't know what I'd do if it weren't for them kids. Just trying to stay strong for them."

And doing a damn fine job of it, I thought.

"Do you have any idea where she might be?" I asked. "No matter how farfetched it is?"

He shook his head and took another sip of his drink.

"Anyone harassing her or threatening her, or was she having conflict with anyone at all?"

He shook his head again and this time added a shrug. "Don't think so. No."

"Did anything out of the ordinary happen in the days or weeks leading up to her disappearance?" I asked. "Anything at all?"

"No. Nothing. Her . . . life—*our* lives were just the same as they had always been. That's why I can't . . . why this makes no sense. I mean . . . who could've . . . done something like this?"

"That's what we're trying to figure out," I said.

"Oh, wait," he said. "There was something. It wasn't like right before she went missing but a few weeks before . . . one of her exes just started harassing her out of the blue."

"Who?"

"Ah, Carl or . . . no . . . Kevin. That's it. Kevin . . . Turner. I thought she said Turnip the first time she said it."

"Kevin Turner was harassing Candace a few weeks before she went missing?" I asked.

"Maybe it was more like a month."

"What was he doing?"

"He'd call here drunk. Follow her around and try to talk to her. Started hanging out at the bar during her shift a lot. Kept asking if Cody was his. One minute he'd tell her they should get back together and raise him right and the next he was saying Cody wasn't his kid and she wasn't gettin' a dime of child support out of him."

Every time Colby and Cody passed by on their bikes, they waved and spoke to me and asked me to watch different tricks they could do. I couldn't help but notice they weren't saying anything to Steve, and I wondered why. Was it because he had seen all their tricks and I was the new audience, or something more sinister? Maybe they knew not to talk to him when he was this far into the bottle of Beam.

"I . . . ain't a bad man," Steve said. "I've . . . had to deal with some . . . shit in my life. Never caught a break. Not one. But that don't keep me from doin' my best. I . . . I damn sure give more than I get. I can tell you that."

"How were things between you and Candace?"

"I didn't have anything to do with this, man. I swear to Christ I didn't. We had our moments. I ain't perfect, but nothin' big. We're no different than anybody else. I'd never hurt her. 'Sides . . . I couldn't. We only got the one car. I was stuck here with the kids. Went to bed early. Wasn't out running my girlfriend off the road and . . . doin' God knows what to her."

"Have you been contacted by the Department of Children and Family Services about Colby and Cody?" I asked.

He nodded. "Case manager came out and talked to us. Asked the kids a bunch of questions. Did psychologicals on them. Said they could stay here for now, but they're looking for a relative they could go live with if their mom doesn't come back soon. Said that if the police ever say that I'm a person of interest they'll be taken from me and put into foster care. So you make sure your dad knows I didn't do it. I don't want to lose these kids. I can't. They're all I got. All I got in the world."

17

B y the time I got home from Steve's, Colby and Cody were there.

I was happy to see them.

I was looking forward to hearing about their day, talking to them about their mom, possibly sharing a pizza with them, and maybe playing some games or just hanging out. They made me less lonely, and I hoped I made them feel cared for and protected and that I provided some stability for them.

"Did your mom ever talk to you about the future?" I asked.

"Like what?" Colby asked.

As usual when talking about her mom, her sad blue eyes grew sadder and bluer.

"Anything," I said. "Plans. Things y'all might do. Places you might go. Anything like that."

We were in my backyard, down by the river. Colby and I were sitting up on the bank in the shade of a cypress tree, Cody playing with action figures in the damp sand at the water's edge.

"She used to always tell me she was sorry for not giving me a better life and tell me she would make it up to me. She'd say 'Baby girl, things are gonna get better. I promise you that. Your mama's gonna do whatever it takes to make it happen.'"

"Do you have any idea what she meant?" I asked. "What she might have been talking about?"

She shrugged her skinny shoulders, her long blond hair spilling off of them as she did, and I was reminded of just how young she really was—something I tended to forget when looking into her eyes or listening to her talk.

"I know she felt bad for stuff I couldn't remember," she said. "I know she was working hard to get us to a better place."

A passing boat sent waves out on either

side of its wake, which by the time they reached the shore were small ripples for Cody's action figures to fight against.

"Did she and Steve get along well?" I asked.

She shook her head. "Not really. She yelled at him a lot."

"Do you remember what about?"

"Not working. Not helping around the house. Drinking too much. Not being better. Doing better."

"How does Steve treat you and Cody?"

"Okay . . . mostly. I guess. He kinda does his own thing. Sleeps a lot. When he's awake he watches TV and drinks."

I thought about that, and wondered what the best thing for Colby and Cody was.

"Do you want to stay with Steve until we find your mom, or would you like to stay somewhere else?"

"Where else would we go?" she asked.

Which broke my heart.

"Well, a relative or a foster parent until—"

"Could we stay here with you?" she asked.

"I wish y'all could," I said, "but . . . the

DCF officials who make the decisions about those sorts of things—"

"Why don't we get to make them?" she asked. "Shouldn't we get to say where we want to stay?"

"Yes, you should," I said, "but the people who make the decisions are there to protect children. Since I'm not related to you and I'm a single man . . . they'd never let me."

"Steve's single and he's a man."

"I know, and I'm not sure how much longer they'll leave y'all with him. Since y'all were living with him before and he's your mom's boyfriend . . . and with your mom being missing . . . they're probably waiting to see . . . waiting for her to be found and come home. I just wanted to make sure you and Cody were all right and to see if you wanted to stay with Steve. If you didn't, I could let them know."

"I guess we better stay where we are for now," she said.

"Y'all are welcome here anytime," I said. "And if you ever need anything at all just let me know."

"I've heard people say that the longer

somebody is missing . . . the more chances that they're probably . . . dead."

I paused for a moment.

I wanted to give her something that I couldn't—the promise of a happy ending. Since I couldn't do that, I could treat her with the respect she deserved and try to leave her with some semblance of hope.

Before I could say anything, she spoke again.

"I want to know the truth," she said. "I really do."

"I'm not going to give up until I find your mom," I said. "And I have every hope of finding her alive. I really think that statistics or other people's opinions don't matter, because every case is different. And they're not going to change what happens in your mom's case. That's the truth."

"I'm not sure it is, John, but . . . okay."

"Are y'all hungry?" I asked. "I could order a pizza."

"Do you ever eat anything else?" she asked. "If you'll get some groceries I'll cook —or teach you how."

"I can cook," I said.

"What?"

"All sorts of things," I said. "I grill a mean steak. I cook a good burger. I can make spaghetti, tacos."

"John," she said in the same voice she would use to scold Cody, "grilling a steak and three things with hamburger meat isn't 'all sorts of things.' It's probably not even cooking."

18

N ights were the worst.

The tin man alone in his tin house.

Loneliness, fear, isolation, guilt. An unquiet mind.

The inability to sleep.

After Colby and Cody left, I had attended an AA meeting, driving to the next county to ensure anonymity. It had helped, but not enough. I returned home and, in the absence of the prospect of sex with anyone other than myself, went jogging.

At midnight I had turned off the lights.

That's when the neon lights inside my head came on.

Thankfully it wasn't long before the phone rang.

"This the chaplain what work for the Potter prison?" an elderly black woman's voice asked. I could hear a loud television and a dog barking in the background.

"Yes, ma'am, it is. John Jordan."

"This is Miss Jenkins. Ike Johnson's aunt."

"Yes ma'am. I'm so sorry about Ike."

"Thank you. We plannin' the funeral and wondered if you would do it."

I was stunned.

"We not really church peoples," she said.

I'm not either, I thought.

"Ike's grandma, Miss Winger, said you's real nice to her."

I had spoken to Grandma Winger earlier that morning to tell her that her grandson, the one she had raised like a son, had been killed. At the time, I thought he was killed while trying to escape. She refused to believe it. She said that they were coming to visit him this Saturday, and he knew it. According to her, his current life was the best one he'd ever had.

"When is the funeral?" I asked.

"Saturday, if you's able to make it. Can you do it Saturday?"

"Yes, I can. I will."

I rolled over after hanging the phone on its cradle and stared up at the ceiling. It hadn't changed.

The breeze outside caused the aluminum of the trailer to bend in and out, making the sound of a whip cracking.

I sat up.

I lay back down.

I decided to get up and work on Ike's funeral some.

I stumbled down the hallway into the living room and made some notes.

Preparing the funeral sermon of a stranger killed under suspicious circumstances was challenging. I grew weary, but I still couldn't sleep.

On my way back to bed, I stopped by the bathroom.

Looking in the mirror, I discovered I looked as tired as I felt.

As I turned to head back to bed, I noticed a small pile of clothes near the shower. It was about two days' worth. I smiled as I thought of how Susan hated that. Having that thought gave me a strong urge to leave them there, which I only overcame because if I left them in reaction to her, she would still be controlling my life. I bent down and scooped them up, slinging one sock between my legs as I did. When I reached for it, I saw something that stopped my heart.

On the back of my left leg, there was a cut about two inches long.

I dropped the clothes and bent down even farther to take a closer look. It wasn't very deep, but still deep enough for AIDS-infected blood splattered on it to get into my bloodstream.

When did I get it? Was it today or before what happened in the sally port?

For the second time that night, my phone rang.

I rushed to the phone, grabbing the receiver as I climbed into bed.

"John John," the voice said. "John John."

Slightly slurred, slightly desperate, slightly scared.

The voice was the voice I heard within the sound of my own when I had been drinking. It was the voice of my mother, and she only called me John John when she was drunk.

"John John, answer me. Are you there?"

"I'm here."

"They got me locked up again. I'm dying. You've got to come see me soon."

"Mom, you're not dying. It just feels like it. It's withdrawals."

"No . . . you . . . don't understand. I haven't been drinkin'. Come see me. Before it's too late. I love you. I love you, John. You've always been my favorite."

"You tell everybody that when you're drunk."

She started coughing. It sounded as if she dropped the phone. Her act was definitely improving.

It took maybe two minutes, which seemed like thirty, for her to pick up the phone again. When she did, she said, "I've got to see you, son . . . before I die."

"What you've got to do is get sober. I'm hanging up now. Call me when you're sober."

19

The next morning as I was meeting with inmates and opening mail, I received another typed note.

Like before, it was a single piece of typing paper, trifolded, taped, with one typewritten word on the outside: *Chaplain.*

I carefully peeled back the tape and opened it.

I could tell immediately that it was produced by the same typewriter as the other one.

It read, *Chaplain, if you don't back off, I'm going to kill you. Just back off, or you're dead. I will kill you and that girl you love. Killing's better than fucking. I love it. I will probably fuck her and then kill her. But I might kill her then fuck her. Back off!*

The institutional mail was delivered every day but Sunday. The note had probably been sent the previous night. Who was it about? I was in love with Anna, but was it obvious to anyone? The other note had spoken of protection, now this one of threat. Were they about two different women? Anna and who? Sandy Strickland? Who else had I been seen with recently?

My office door opened and Tom Daniels walked in.

I nodded toward one of the chairs across from my desk as I carefully folded the letter and stuck it in my desk drawer.

He sat down.

Looking better than he had yesterday, his face wasn't as red, his eyes not as bloodshot.

He looked down at the clipboard that he was carrying, flipped through a couple of pages, then looked back up at me.

"Look, the warden said we've got to work together. Neither of us is happy about it, but whatcha gonna do, right?"

I knew the warden's words alone were

not enough to bring about this change in him.

"The investigation is more important than our dislike of one another. Wouldn't you agree?"

"I don't dislike you. I'd like to talk with you about what happened."

"I've heard your excuses before."

"I've never offered any excuses. You've only heard things from Susan."

He shook his head. "Don't want to talk about it. Just concentrate on the work. I don't like you, but I can work with anyone."

"I'm sorry for any pain I've caused you or your family. I love Susan. Only want the best for her."

He was unable to hide his obvious awkwardness and discomfort.

"We need to follow up some of the leads that our physical evidence has produced," he said. "You could do some of them without anyone noticing. IG of the department walks in and starts asking questions, people get nervous and clam up."

No wonder he was being civil. He needed my help.

"Like what?" I asked.

"The lab said there were traces of a chemical on Johnson's pants that's used in floor cleaner and wax in medical and dental facilities. We've traced the exact chemical to two types of cleaners manufactured by PRIDE. The cleaners are used in the medical offices, the infirmary, and the dental offices."

"We know he was in the infirmary the night before he was killed."

"But he couldn't get it on him from just being there—even if he fell on a recently mopped floor. Besides, the chemical on his pants had not been diluted. He'd've had to come in contact with an actual bottle of cleaner, and it'd have to have been within a few hours of his death."

"We need to find out if he ever worked with the cleaner or if his uniform was switched with someone else's. Happens a lot. Uniform could've come in contact with the chemical when another inmate was wearing it."

He shook his head. "I doubt it. The chemical had not been through the washer and dryer, and the uniform had his name tag on it. It actually stuck to the spear. How about Medical and Dental?"

"I'll check them again as I can. I have to continue my regular work as well. And I've been asked to do Ike Johnson's funeral on Saturday."

"Find out all you can about him from his family," he said. "They may know something useful and not know they know it."

I nodded.

"I think it's best if we're not seen together. You do those things. I'll talk with Fortner, make him feel a part of the investigation, and continue to check with the lab."

Working together without working together. It was ingenious.

20

Merrill Monroe, my best friend since elementary school, was an African-American correctional officer sergeant in charge of Outside Grounds.

Inmates assigned to his crew were not considered escape risks and were allowed to work outside the gate.

I found him in a garden to the left of the institution, down on his hands and knees showing an inmate just how to plant sugar snap peas.

The light brown sleeves of his short-sleeve CO uniform were stretched tightly over muscular dark brown arms. Every time he moved, his muscles flexed, straining his shirt to the point of ripping.

As he instructed the inmate on exactly how to do his job, he spoke in slow, even tones. I had seen him stare down a gang of inmates, two with shanks, the same way. I had also seen him wipe out an entire gang by himself, never raising his voice and never acting as if it required much effort either.

"Sarge, you got a minute?" I asked as I came up behind him.

He stood, nodding at me and pointing at the row of peas to the inmate.

We walked away from the garden and the inmates working there for some privacy.

"I was thinking of planting some sugar snap peas and needed some help."

"Shee-it. Your ass ever planted anything in your life?"

"Not too late to start, is it? Really am about to put some sod around my trailer."

"Want some advice?" he said.

"From an expert like yourself? Of course."

"Put the green side up," he said, a broad

smile creeping across his face, revealing his startling white teeth.

We were both silent a moment.

He glanced back in the direction of the garden. I could tell he was not happy with how the inmates were planting the peas.

"It's hard to get good help these days," I said.

"Yeah. Speaking of which, I heard about what you did in the sally port on Tuesday. Pretty impressive for a skinny white boy."

"I'm not skinny," I protested. "I'm fit."

"You's fit before all that shit in Atlanta," he said. "Now you skinny."

He stood directly in front of me, positioning himself between me and the sun, the shadow he cast keeping me from needing the shades I had left in my office. He was always doing things like that and never mentioning it.

I could see my reflection in his glasses. I looked distorted, like my face was too big for my head and body. Merrill towered over my six feet by about four inches, totally eclipsing the sun.

"Anyway," he continued, "you did good.

Showed some of these rednecks that a man can be civilized and have balls too."

"Did Johnson work for you?"

"On paper."

My eyebrows shot up. "Oh really?"

"He was assigned to Outside Grounds but never came. Each month I got a note from Captain Skipper saying he using Johnson other places, just go ahead and give him credit for working out here."

"And you did it?" I asked, a little surprised.

"Captain say do it, I do it," he said, falling back into his favorite dialect for expressing his frustration. "I not smart enough to think for myself. Don't ask no questions. No sir."

Merrill thought for himself all right, and asked plenty of questions. As smart as any man I'd ever met, Merrill had been unable to attend college. Instead he had spent much of his time at the public library and already had a much better education than most college graduates.

"Did he ever show up out here for work?" I asked.

"When he was first assigned here. Came

out about three times. Didn't do a damn thing. Worried about his fingernails and hair too much."

"Oh yeah?"

"Inmates called him Go-down 'cause he a go down on anybody."

I nodded, thinking about the picture developing of little Ike Johnson.

"You tell me anything about Hardy? CO who works nights in the infirmary."

"Ex-military," he said. "Still in the reserves. Hell of a good officer. Smart. Tough. Fair. He not as good as me, but . . . he's good."

"Pretty confident for a black man named after a dead white woman."

He ran his hand across his short hair and then started patting it. "With good reason."

"Anything else about Johnson you can think of?"

"Didn't know him that well, But I'll tell you who did. Inmate named Willie Baker. Probably the oldest homosexual on the compound. Hell, maybe even in the world."

"The one they call Grandma?" I asked.

He smiled. "Yeah," he said with surprise and amusement. "Chaplain got the 4-1-1."

"That's me, Mr. Information. But it's not the 4-1-1, but the 9-1-1 that concerns me. You ever get a request from Johnson? Was it typed?"

He shook his head. "Nigga couldn't read or write."

21

Blue movement everywhere.

The compound pulsing with energy.

Inmates laughing, yelling, talking, walking, playing, lining up, gathering in small groups, moving. Always moving.

Inmates on the compound were in perpetual motion.

Above it all, the hot July sun was unrelenting, unforgiving. The only shade was provided by four pavilions. But even if they blocked the sun, they were impotent against the heat.

The heat was stifling, thick and difficult to breathe.

As I walked through the open population, I was again reminded that I was a stranger in a strange land. This was their world. Most of the inmates treated me like a servant at a dinner party.

Passing through the lower compound, I made my way down to the rec yard where inmates were playing basketball, softball, lifting weights, and walking around the track —all beneath the clear blue sky.

I found Willie at the far end of the field, sitting on the ground, leaning up against the back of the softball fence.

He looked about a hundred and fifty. His gray hair, what little there was, made a nearly complete circle around the crown of his head. His eyes were hollow. His stubbly gray beard sporadically covered his gaunt face, dipping down in the recesses of his cheeks because he had no teeth.

If he was in any way effeminate, you couldn't tell just by looking at him. Of course, if he was alive, you couldn't tell it just by looking at him either.

He sat with two other men, both in their twenties, both as feminine as most females I'd ever seen, more so than many.

I squatted down in front of Willie. "Mind if I ask you a few questions?"

Willie's expression didn't change.

"Grandma," the inmate to his left said in a high falsetto voice, "Chaplain want to talk whichya."

Willie didn't respond.

A gray officer's station building stood in the center of the rec yard. Part of it was open, housing free weights and Ping-Pong tables. Scattered all around it were card tables where small groups of inmates played checkers, chess, and dominoes.

"Grandma," he said again, this time patting his cheek as he did, "wake up, old girl. They's a man what wants to talk whichya."

Willie's eyes drifted slowly back down to earth, landing somewhere in my vicinity. Then he said in a soft, airy voice, "Who—" he breathed out and paused as if this would require the last bit of life that was left in him "—is . . . it?"

"It's the chaplain. The new one," he said.

"The fine one," the other one said.

Willie leaned down and whispered something in the ear of the inmate to his left.

He was obviously the spokesperson for the group. His name tag read Jefferson.

"Grandma wants to know if you think homosexuals have no hope where God concerned."

"I don't think anybody has no hope where God is concerned."

Willie leaned down again and whispered something else in Jefferson's ear.

Around us the other inmates on the rec yard were loud and active, sounding like children on a playground. And, in many ways, that's what they were.

"Grandma say you all right," Jefferson said. "Whatcha wanna know?"

"Everything there is to know about Ike Johnson."

"Grandma say he dead. What else they to know?" Jefferson said after receiving instructions from Grandma to do so.

"I want to know all about him while he was alive so I can find out why he was killed."

Beyond the blacktop court where young black men played full-court basketball like they did in Miami, the elderly inmates played horseshoes like they did in retirement homes in Sarasota. Past them, the young white inmates played volleyball the way they did on Panama City Beach. Yet, beyond all of this, the wall of chain-link fence and razor wire served as an ominous reminder of exactly which part of Florida this was.

"Grandma say he a real ho. Do anything. Sooner or later his kind always gets stuck. Grandma say everybody think he belonged to Jacobson, but he didn't. Grandma say he belonged to another inmate, and they both belong to a cop."

"A correctional officer here at the prison?" I asked.

"Yeah. But the point is he wasn't loyal. He'd do anything anytime. He also run his big mouth."

"What else can you tell me?" I asked.

"Grandma say that all she can say, 'cause she ain't got a big mouth."

I thought about all the names that I had come across so far in this investigation. I wanted to ask him about at least one of them.

"Can you tell me who Johnson's real old man was?" I asked.

"Can't say," Jefferson said.

"What about Captain Skipper?" I asked.

"Grandma say he won't say nothin' about that redneck son of a bitch," Jefferson said.

"Okay, what about Allen Jones, the inmate who works in the infirmary?"

Again the whisper, again Jefferson with the response. "Say all he know is he well looked out for. He in love with them nurses."

"How about a young officer named Shutt?" I continued.

"Must be new, 'cause Grandma don't know him," Jefferson said.

"Anything else you can tell me that might help me find out who killed Johnson and why?"

"Grandma say it come down to three things. Sex. Drugs. Rock 'n roll. Everything in here do."

22

"Who can I get drugs from?" I asked.

"Things already gotten that bad?" Anna said.

She was wearing a colorful jumper with blooming spring flowers all over it. It fit nicely, though not too nicely. Never too nicely in here. Her long brown hair was worn down in long, looping waves.

"If an inmate wants to buy drugs on the compound," I said, "how does he do it?"

I was seated across from her desk in a blue plastic chair that sloped down to the left.

Behind her, through the window, I could

see inmates mowing dead grass. The sun had taken a toll on everything this year, but the grass most of all. The waves of heat made the inmates look as if they were many miles rather than a few hundred feet away.

"Well, let's see," she said, narrowing her eyes and tapping her pencil on her forehead. "First he would have to have something to buy them with. This could be cash from an outside account, personal property to trade —say, a watch, a ring, or canteen items—or he could be willing to do something—sex, a hit, a favor."

"Do many of them have what it takes to buy drugs?" I asked.

"Not many have cash, but nearly all have something of value—we're talking about the trading of goods and services."

"Just how available are drugs on the compound?" I asked.

"Not as much as you might think after working here and seeing all the crime, but a whole hell of a lot more than a person on the street would think."

"How does it get in?"

"Some of it's homemade. We have chemicals here and a pharmacy. Usually though, the homemade stuff is liquor. Most of the drugs come in because someone brings them in—family and friends during visitation, or COs or staff smuggle it in to sell or trade."

"What about screenings?" I asked.

"Officially, they'll tell you we do random drug screenings. Unofficially, most of them are conducted after we receive a tip from another inmate. Of course, after an inmate tests positive once, he is watched more closely."

"How could Johnson have had more than one kind of drug in his system when the tests done on him in both Confinement and Medical came back negative?"

She thought about it for a moment.

"I can only think of three possibilities. Inmate somehow faked the test—traded urine with someone or something like that. It was an honest mistake by the officer doing the test. Or, someone was looking out for him."

We fell silent a moment.

I tried to process and piece together all the information I had received recently.

"Have you received any threats lately?" I asked.

She smiled. "You mean in addition to the normal stuff?"

"Yeah."

"No. Why?"

"Just curious," I said.

"You're never *just* anything," she said. "Especially *just* curious."

"Just be careful."

"I always am," she said.

"Extra careful for a while, okay?"

She nodded slowly. "Okay."

I told her about the notes I'd been receiving.

Before she could respond, her phone rang.

She answered it.

"It's for you," she said after putting the call on hold. "Says it's urgent, but she'll only talk to you in your office."

"Who is it?"

"Molly Thomas."

"Okay," I said, standing. "Will you give me a few minutes to get to my office, and transfer it?"

23

When I got back to the chapel my phone was ringing. Fumbling with the keys, I rushed in just as it stopped. I sat down at my desk and less than a minute later it started again.

"Chaplain, this is Molly Thomas," she said in a soft voice.

Molly Thomas was the devoted wife of an inmate here at PCI named Anthony Thomas. She was devoted enough to her husband and their relationship to move up from South Florida when he was transferred here. She rented a small trailer in a trailer park not far from mine and visited her husband six hours every Saturday and six hours every Sunday.

"Hey, Molly. How's it going?" I asked.

"Not very good right now. I was wondering if I might talk with you?" she asked hesitantly.

"Of course, you know that," I said.

"Not over the phone."

"Why don't you come to the institution this afternoon? We can meet in the administration building."

The administration and training buildings were the only ones not behind the fence.

"Can we meet somewhere in town?"

"There's a conference room I use sometimes at the sheriff's station. We can meet there if you like."

"I . . . I can't really meet you there either."

"How about the Methodist Church on Main Street at one o'clock?"

"That would be great."

"I'll see you there."

After we hung up, Mr. Smith ambled in with some inmate requests and passes for me.

I looked through them. There was nothing urgent.

"Have a seat," I said. "Mind if I ask you a few more questions?"

"No suh. Don't mind a'tall."

"I'm tryin' to find out who supplies drugs on the compound."

"Probably the biggest supplier that is a inmate is Jasper Evans."

"Really?"

"Yes suh."

"The inmate who directs the choir and never misses chapel is the biggest supplier on the compound?"

He nods. "'Fraid so. He sing like an angel but sling dope like the devil."

24

When I reached the First United Methodist Church of Pottersville, Molly Thomas was waiting on me.

The red-brick and white-trim church looked as much like an old schoolhouse as anything else.

Molly sat in her car, an older dark brown Ford Taurus, with her window rolled down. Her auburn hair was moist, and sweat trickled down the sides of her cheeks. Her green eyes, aided by colored contact lenses, looked like the Gulf after a summer rain.

Glancing around nervously, she got out of the car.

I got out too, but without the nervous glances. Later, I realized I should have been glancing.

"Are you okay?" I asked.

"I'm scared out of my mind. I don't know what to do. I need your help."

"We can use the pastor's office. He's at lunch right now," I said, walking toward the office at the rear of the church.

Pastor Clydesdale's office was way too small for his library, books spilling out of the three large bookshelves, piled on the floor, stacked on his desk and filing cabinet. The floor was covered with a dark green shag carpet from deep in the 1970s. A small window air conditioner, which was not in a window at all but in an oversized hole in the wall, pushed the sweet smell of pipe smoke around the room.

I sat in the pastor's seat, an old, wooden swivel desk chair with casters on its legs.

Molly sat on an old couch that was covered with a thin rust-colored bedspread and sloped down at the rear, making her appear six inches shorter than she really was.

"I'm taking an awful risk in talking to

you," she said. "I think I can trust you, but I'm not sure."

"If you have any reservations, I would encourage you to speak with someone you know better and can trust more."

"I don't know anyone. I am all alone down here. Out of options."

Her auburn hair and green eyes were striking, though it was obvious neither were completely natural.

"Down here? I thought you were from South Florida."

"No, I'm from Michigan. We were in Miami about to leave for a two-week cruise when Tony was arrested."

I nodded. "If you want to talk with me, there are some things you should know first. I will keep confidential anything you say unless to do so would cause harm to you, someone else, or the security of the institution. Also, we are not alone here."

She startled. Sitting up, looking around.

"No one is listening in on us. We have privacy. Just wanted you to know. It's for my protection and yours."

"Who's here?" she asked, looking around the room.

"The pastor is having his lunch in the other office."

"Makes me trust you even more. The thing is . . . Tony's been doing real good. I was worried about him. He's not like those other men. But he's doing good. A lot better than I ever would've thought."

"Is that why you stayed around? To look out for him?"

"I thought if I was here, he wouldn't feel so alone, and that might help him make it."

"And it has."

"It has. Or had. But about a month ago, Tony started acting real sure of himself, like he didn't need me anymore. He said that the most powerful man at the institution was looking out for him and that his last year would be cake. He was so cocky I couldn't stand it. I hate it when he gets like that."

"He say who the man was?" I asked.

"No. Never did. But when I'd go to visit on the weekends he'd have all kinds of money to spend at the canteen and he'd give me little presents. A nice watch. Earrings. A bracelet. Also started putting money in my bank account. Large deposits."

"He say where it came from?" I asked.

"Only thing he ever said was the skipper took care of his mates."

She sniffled and blinked and began to cry.

I handed her a tissue from the box on the desk.

"Last Saturday when I was visiting he said he had something very special planned for us this week. That he'd call and for me not to be scared. I had no idea what it could be, but I was excited. I got a call from him Tuesday night saying for me to come to the institution. Said he'd worked it out for us to be alone. I was scared. I knew it was against the rules. But I went. When I got there, the officer at the control room said Captain Skipper was expecting me. They didn't have me sign in or anything. When I got into the sally port, a big man in a white shirt met me and escorted me to the chapel."

"The *chapel*?"

"Yeah. No one was there. It was very dark. The officer told me to go into the sanctuary and wait for Tony. When I got in there Tony was waiting for me."

She began to tremble, her tears coming harder.

"He took me from behind, like he was attacking me. He grabbed me and slung me to the ground. At first I didn't know who it was, but then he started talking to me. It was . . . He was like an animal. I tried to turn around, but he wouldn't let me. He had my jeans off before I knew it. Whispering the most . . . explicit things in my ear. Things he's never said before."

"Why don't you pause for a moment," I said, giving her the box of tissues.

"I . . . have to . . . go on. Or I . . . won't finish. It's so . . . He attacked me. There's no other word for it. He's my husband and I wanted to . . . I was there because I . . . wanted to be, but . . . not like that. Not . . . It felt like he put his fist . . . his whole fist inside me. He was completely out of control. It wasn't like my Tony at all. Then, he . . . he . . . sodomized me."

"I am so sorry," I said.

"I'm . . . no saint. Tony and I have had sex in every way . . . but . . . He raped me."

"I'm so, so sorry."

"He hurt me," she said. "Not too bad . . . physically, but real bad emotionally. He . . . The worst thing was before he was even through, the big officer in the white shirt and two others in brown shirts came in and pulled him off of me and cuffed him. I think they had been watching the whole time. I've never been so humiliated in my life. One of 'em jerked me up, told me to get dressed, and then led me to the gate. I was so upset and disoriented . . . I don't remember much else . . . except when I reached my trailer and got out, a truck pulled in behind me. It was the big officer in the white shirt. He . . . He was running toward me. I dropped my keys, but thankfully I had left the door unlocked. I ran in and locked the door just before he reached it. He tried it. It was locked. Then it hit me—my keys—they were out there on the ground. I put the dead bolt on and the chain. He came back and unlocked the knob, but couldn't open the door because of the dead bolt. He started kicking the door. I ran into the kitchen and called 9-1-1. When I got back he was gone. This is the first time I've come out of the house since then."

"You know the name of the big officer in the white shirt?" I asked.

"No. I assumed it was Skipper, but I don't know. God, he's a psychopath. You should have heard him laughing at me just before they pulled Tony off me."

"You ever seen him before?" I asked.

"No, never. I take it that he is either a captain or a lieutenant because of the color of his shirt, but I couldn't see his collar."

"What time did all this take place?" I asked.

"I'm not sure," she said.

"It's very important. Was it before or after eleven?"

"Oh, after. It was way after eleven. Why?"

"The shift changes at eleven. So does the shift OIC. While you were at the institution, how many different officers did you see?" I asked.

"One in the control room. Three in the chapel."

"Wonder how many saw you."

She shuddered at that.

"You willing to come with me to report this to the warden, the inspector, and the sheriff?"

"What? No. Absolutely not. I'm . . . No. Never."

"I have to report it."

"I don't. I'm not. I'm gonna work on getting Tony transferred and never come back here again."

"But—"

"Don't even think about involving me. If anybody from the prison or the cops ask, I'm gonna swear that none of this ever happened."

"Then why'd you tell me?"

"I want you to check on Tony, take care of him, help him. Protect him from those officers."

"Be a lot easier to do with your statement."

She shook her head. "I can't. I . . . just . . . can't."

I nodded. "Okay. Want me to get the sheriff to assign someone to watch you while we work on this?"

"You can do that? You're something else, Chaplain."

"No. Just related to him."

25

"What exactly are we doing here?" Anna asked.

We were sitting at the large conference table in the medical break room.

Designed more for meetings than breaks, it was a conference room with a Coke machine. The corridor ending here led past the steel doors of the suicide cells on one side and the glass walls of the infirmary on the other.

I was drinking a can of Florida orange juice, she a Diet Coke.

"We're taking a break," I said.

She looked confused.

"We're state employees. We take lots of them."

"Oh, we do?"

"Okay, so we never do," I said, "but today we're turning over a new leaf."

I had called her just after returning from my meeting with Molly Thomas, and just before calling both Dad about assigning a deputy to watch her and Tom Daniels to fill him in and ask about getting the FDLE crime scene technicians to examine the chapel floor for trace evidence that might verify Molly's story.

Anna sipped some more of her Diet Coke, then raised the can and said, "To taking more breaks."

I held my juice up and we clinked cans.

"What we're *really* doing here," I whispered, "is looking for clues."

Her eyes widened. "Clues? Cool. Am I playing Watson to your Holmes? Actually, I should be Nancy Drew or your Girl Friday."

She could be my Girl Monday through Sunday. That would be just fine with me.

"I've been thinking more about the notes I've been receiving. I really think they're about you."

"Could be."

"It's obvious how much I care about you, and the letters are coming from within the institution. Somebody who has seen us together . . ."

She nodded. "What do you want me to do?"

"Don't go anywhere alone. Let me or Merrill or someone you trust be with you. Just take extra precautions for the next little while."

"I can do that."

"Thanks."

We drank a little more.

"I need to look in some of the rooms down here, and I need someone to cause a distraction and keep lookout."

"Why don't you create a distraction and keep lookout while I look for clues?" "I don't think the officer in the infirmary would find me as distracting as you."

She smiled. "Don't sell yourself short."

While she plied her charms to distract the infirmary officer, I went to take a look in the caustic storage closets for the cleaning chemicals found on Johnson's uniform.

Both were locked.

I reached in my back pocket, whipped out my wallet, and withdrew the Visa card. Sliding it down the side of the doorjamb, the door opened easily. Too easily. Someone had done this before—many times.

The first closet had a single metal shelf that looked like it should have been in someone's garage. It was filled with boxes of garbage bags, paper towels, toilet paper, and rubber gloves. The bottom shelf was filled with white plastic bottles of PRIDE chemicals: wax, stripper, floor cleaner, glass cleaner, and two cans of the spray that killed HIV and hepatitis on contact.

Getting down on my hands and knees, I took a closer look, resisting the urge to touch anything. When I moved to the side of the shelf, I saw it. On the back side there was a bottle of cleaner leaking, the liquid standing around the base of the bottle, the shelf, and the floor.

Walking back up toward the front, I saw Allen Jones, the elderly inmate orderly mopping the floor.

He was so quiet, his moves so understated, I wouldn't have heard him if he hadn't been whistling—a soft, airy whistle version of "As Time Goes By."

When I arrived at the infirmary control room, Anna was still beguiling Ron Straub.

"How's it going?" I said.

"Fine," he said, not bothering to mask his irritation at the intrusion.

"Do you have an inmate in the infirmary named Anthony Thomas?"

"Jones," he yelled to the orderly out in the hallway, "wasn't Thomas put in Confinement Tuesday morning?"

"Yes, sir," Jones said.

"He's in Confinement," Straub said.

"Thank you. I'll see him over there."

When I began to leave, he smiled.

When Anna joined me, he stopped.

"WHAT'D YOU FIND?" Anna asked when we were seated in her office again.

"Maybe where the body was stored until the trash was taken out."

"Where?"

"In one of the caustic storage rooms at the end of the hallway past the infirmary. It'd be the perfect place. That hallway is almost always empty and very few people use that closet."

"What made you look in there in the first place?"

I told her.

"And asking about Thomas?" she said. "Was that just about what Molly told you or do you think he has something to do with what happened to Johnson?"

"Both," I said. "Maybe."

She gave me a big smile.

"What?"

"Some men will brag when given the opportunity to do so to an attentive female."

"I've heard about that."

"I gave Ron my full attention and he told some tales—one of them about an inmate having an affair with a nurse."

"Thomas?" I asked

"Thomas," she said.

"Did he say which nurse?"

"I don't think he knows, but I soon will."

26

I was in my office making notes on the case when Merrill walked in.

"'Sup?" he said when he was seated in front of me.

I shook my head. "You'd have to ask somebody else. You're looking at the man who knows the least about the way things work around here."

"It a different world. But you a quick study. You rounded up the usual suspects?"

"Working on it."

"How many brothers on the list?" he said.

"Besides you? Only have one suspect of African descent."

"Everybody of African descent. We the first people on Earth."

"True."

"Nigga got a name?"

"Name and a number," I said. "Allen Jones. Works in the infirmary. Has no real motive that I can see, but he gathers and takes out the trash. Also has access to a typewriter. Most inmates don't. But Nurse Anderson says he didn't take the trash out on Tuesday. Speaking of . . . what can you tell me about Shutt?"

"Not much," he said. "He's pretty new. Seems okay. He a suspect?"

"He picked up the trash, and he's the one who actually did the deed."

"Shook him up like hell too, though, didn't it?"

"Maybe. Certainly seemed to."

"Who else?"

"Jacobson, of course. Skipper."

"He probably involved somehow. Bastard bad all the way down to his black heart."

I told him what Molly Thomas had told me.

Merrill shook his head. "Like I said."

"Seems we're surrounded by badness," I

said. "I think Anna might be in danger. I've been getting threatening letters and I think they're about her."

"You told her?" he asked.

"Yeah. Would you keep an eye on her?"

"Always do. Will watch her with both now."

SHORTLY AFTER MERRILL LEFT, Mr. Smith brought Sandy Strickland in to see me.

It was a pleasant surprise.

"Just wanted to stop by and check on you."

"Thank you. That's very kind of you. I am anxious to know the results of the test. Found a cut on my leg last night. Don't know when I got it, but..."

"I know waiting's the worst part, but I really don't think you have anything to worry about. Even if you did have a cut on your leg, his blood would have had to seep all the way through your pants."

"I know. I'm just..."

She frowns and shakes her head. "I'm so sorry. We're at such high risk here. It's . . .

Anyway, call me if it gets too much for you. But try not to worry. I'm sure you're fine."

She stood to leave.

I stood and came around my desk to walk her out.

When I reached her, she kissed me briefly on the lips.

"See?" she said. "I'm so convinced you haven't been infected that I'm willing to kiss you."

I started to say something but she leaned in and kissed me again.

The second kiss started out friendly enough, but grew deeper and more passionate as she lingered.

"Sorry," she said. "I got caught up, but would I do that if I thought you were infected?"

27

"Chaplain?" Stone was saying.

"Sorry," I said. "I was just thinking."

Something had been said, something I missed while I was lost in thought—Anthony and Molly Thomas, Ike Johnson, Sandy Strickland, Anna, Laura Mathers, HIV, AIDS, blood, and murder all swirling around in my head.

Tom Daniels and I were in Stone's office to give him an update.

"About what the inspector said?" Stone asked.

"What'd he say?" I asked.

Stone frowned deeply.

"That Officer Shutt has been written up several times on accusations of brutality toward inmates—every one of them black," Daniels said.

"What has been done? Did you know about this?" I asked Stone.

He frowned at me again and shook his head.

"Not much has been done," Daniels said, "as you would expect, because the grievances have been written by inmates. It seems that on a couple of occasions, he was reprimanded by his supervisor."

"That'll teach him," I said.

Stone frowned at me again. The man was nothing if not consistent.

"You both know what it's like," Daniels said. "We get grievances on staff members all the time. Some inmates spend all their time writing grievances. Good officers and staff get written up all the time. It's almost impossible to know. There's nobody in the entire department who hasn't been written up by some inmate for some silly something."

I shook my head.

Daniels said, "What?"

"There's a difference in frivolous inmate

grievances and a pattern of abuse against a single race."

"There's no evidence of that," he said.

"But there's accusation and it should have been investigated."

"How many reports of abuse has he received?" Edward Stone said.

"Twelve," Daniels said.

"How many years with the department?" I asked.

"Less than two."

"Watch him very closely, Inspector. If he's guilty, I want his ass."

"Were any of the grievances filed by Ike Johnson?" I asked.

Daniels nodded.

Edward Stone's eyebrows peeked several inches above his glasses. "Seems significant."

"I'll look into it and him more," Daniels said. "About the sleeping pills . . . Doc says they were not given by syringe or in food. So it seems Johnson just took them. Some of the capsules weren't even fully dissolved yet."

"Suicide?" Stone asked, his voice sounding hopeful.

"It's at least a possibility."

"But it rules out staff and officers," Stone said.

I shook my head.

Daniels said, "It probably does remove the suspicion from the employees, yes, sir."

"What about Skipper?" I said.

"I've initiated an investigation into him," Daniels said.

"Shouldn't he be suspended pending the investigation?" I said.

"Because of the accusation of an inmate's wife?" he said.

"A very serious accusation," I said. "And she's not the only one saying he's dirty and brutal. Several staff members have said it too."

"He may be dirty. If he is, I'm gonna take him down," Daniels said. "But for now I'm leaving him in place while I investigate and or build a case against him."

"Which is your call—"

"You damn right it is."

"—but how many more people will he brutalize or kill while you do?"

28

The air in Confinement was ten degrees hotter than the air outside and lacked the breeze.

Body odor and the smell of sleep hung in the air like a fog, so thick as to be visible.

It was quiet, as if the heat had zapped all of everyone's energy.

When I reached Anthony Thomas's cell, he was kneeling at the food tray slot as if he had been expecting me.

"How are you, Anthony? I asked.

He shook his head slightly and stared up at me, trying to focus on me. His movements were slow and unsteady. When his eyes finally came within the vicinity of mine, he grinned with way too much familiarity.

"Hello, John," he said.

It was the first time an inmate had ever called me by my first name.

"How are you feeling?" I asked.

"Top of the world. Top of the fuckin' world. You?"

"Looks like maybe you might have left this world," I said.

He didn't respond.

"How's Molly?" I asked.

"Molly. Molly. Molly," he said. "Molly is my wife, but you, you are my true love."

"Me?"

"Sure you are. I really love you, man."

He was so high I had nothing to lose. I probably wouldn't get good answers but it didn't mean I couldn't ask good questions.

"I know Molly is your wife but I hear you have a girlfriend here at the prison?"

"I have lots of friends."

"Like who?"

"You're my friend, John. Ike was my friend, but he's not my friend anymore. He's dead. He's like on a different plane now."

"Tell me about Ike?" I asked.

"He was ... my friend."

"I think we've established that. Anything else you can add?"

"He was a good friend. A real sweetheart. I wish they didn't kill him."

"Who?"

"That pig fucker Skipper. He's ..."

"He's what?" I asked.

"Head pig fucker. Runs this place. He's the skipper of this ship."

"What makes you say that?" I asked.

"Does what he wants to, man. Uses ... abuses ... Nobody can stop him. Stone's scared of him ... My name should be Stoned."

"How about Molly? Does Skipper use or abuse her?"

At that his face clouded over and he began to cry. First small tears, followed hard on by bigger and bigger ones. "Fat pig fucker son of a bitch. Gonna kill him."

He leaned his head against the steel door and cried some more. In a few minutes, he was snoring.

I walked back down the hallway toward the desk to speak to the officer seated there. On my way by Jacobson's cell, I looked in. He was completely naked, standing in the center of the cell with a full erection.

When he saw me, he ran to the door and began to shout, "I'M THE DEVIL'S SON. I'M THE DEVIL'S SON."

"I'm sure he's real proud," I said, continuing to walk.

"Got a question for you," I said to the officer when I reached his desk.

"Shoot," he said.

"Is he on medication?"

"Jacobson, yeah. Sleeping pills. But between you and me, he don't take nearly enough of 'em. Wish he'd sleep all the time."

"I meant Anthony Thomas," I said. "He's high as hell."

"Thomas?" He shrugged. "Beats me. Better ask the nurse."

"Which one?" I said, finding it odd he knew Jacobson was on sleeping pills and didn't know what was making Anthony Thomas float around his cell.

"Any of them can tell you, I'm sure, but he sees Anderson the most, I think."

"Thank you," I said, and walked out.

.   .   .

I WAS WALKING BACK toward the chapel when I saw her.

Well, not her, but her truck. It was headed toward the warehouse. And in an instant, so was I.

When I reached the warehouse the truck was still there, backed up to the loading dock, its flashers blinking.

I walked up the ramp and entered the cargo bay.

When I stepped inside, I could see her and the warehouse supervisor in his office. I walked over as nonchalantly as I could, but it probably resembled running.

"Hello, Chaplain, what brings you out here?" Rick Spawn said when I stepped into the doorway of his office.

Before I could answer, I glanced in her direction.

"Hey there, Chaplain JJ," she said with a big smile.

"Hey," I said.

"Good to see you again," she said enthusiastically.

"You two know each other?" Rick asked.

"I bought the chaplain a pizza the other night," Laura said. "It wasn't a date or anything, but I think he's smitten. Probably here to ask me out. You think I should go?"

"I think you should go out with me," he said.

"I don't date married men," she said. "Besides, he's cute. In a discarded-mutt sort of way."

We turned to walk out together.

"Aren't you forgetting something?" Rick asked.

"What's that?"

"What'd you come out here for?"

"Just stopped by to say hi. You know, making the rounds."

"It's obvious he came out here to see me," Laura said. "When he saw my truck, he nearly ran across the compound."

I smiled as I turned to leave. "And it was worth it. For the abuse if nothing else." I walked out ahead of her.

"Wait up," she said as she caught up to me. "You're not going to break your neck running over here and then not even ask me out, are you?"

"Think about it," I said, flashing her another smile.

"Well, hell. My mom would die if she

heard this, but . . . I guess I'll just have to ask you out."

"Don't do that. I couldn't bear to be the cause of your mother's departing. Would you go out with me? I'll pick you up Saturday morning."

"Saturday morning? The hell kind of date is that?"

"I have to go to Tallahassee. You can come along and we'll make a day of it."

"Doing what?" she asked.

"It'll be a surprise."

"Okay. I'll try anything once."

"Where do I pick you up?"

"You going to the jamboree? Find me at the game, and I'll tell you where to pick me up. And if you lose that little priest outfit you have on, I just might let you help me chaperone my little sister's jamboree dance."

29

When I got home Colby and Cody were waiting for me. I had just dropped by the barn where their mom's abandoned car had been found and where now cadaver dogs were searching for her body, and it made me want to grab them and hug them and hold them but I resisted that urge and instead asked about their day and offered to take them to get ice cream and rent a movie.

As we were about to walk out the door, my phone rang.

"I have phone records," Kimmy said. "I don't know how you pulled that off, but I'm glad you did 'cause guess what I found?"

Cupping the receiver with my hand, I asked the kids to wait for me out front.

"How did you pull it off, by the way?" she asked. "They were just in my cubby with my name on them."

"I guarantee what you found is far more interesting," I said. "Let's talk about that instead."

"Neither Steve nor Candace were stepping out on the other," she said. "Or at least if they were they never called their lovers and their lovers never called them. The sad reality is they never make or receive many calls at all. They get more sales calls than anything else. That in itself would be enough to make me run away."

"Hopefully Candace had a greater tolerance for annoyances than you do," I said. "So now that you've told me what you didn't find . . . how about telling me what you did?"

"She made several calls to a women's shelter in Panama City Beach called Hope House."

"There it is," I said. "That's it."

"You knew we'd find something like that?" she asked.

"No, just hoped. You wanna ride out there with me?"

"Well I doubt they'll let you in otherwise."

"Why?" I asked. "I exude hope."

"You have a penis," she said.

"It exudes hope too."

As COLBY, Cody, and I stepped out of Ronnie B's Munchies and Movies with our ice cream and videos, Kevin Turner and Mason Kelley were standing there.

They both had the wild, wide-eyed, emaciated, feral look of users who are way, way down the rabbit hole.

"Hey, little man," Kevin said to Cody.

Cody could tell there was something unpredictable and menacing about the man and wasn't sure what to do. He looked at me.

"It's rude not to speak when you're spoken to," Kevin said. "'Specially by an adult. Raised right, you'd know that."

I looked down at Cody. "You did just right, buddy."

It was late evening and downtown was

deserted, and if it had cooled off any since midday, I couldn't tell it.

I looked back up and locked eyes with Kevin. Twitching from whatever he was on, he quickly looked away.

"Obviously, he's been taught not to talk to strangers," I said.

"Don't know about all that," he said. "Who the hell're you? You a stranger to me."

I looked down at Colby and Cody again. "Y'all go wait in the truck for me," I said. "I'll be there in a minute. Everything's *okay*."

Colby took Cody's hand and led him the short distance to my truck.

"'Course everything's okay," Kevin said. "What's wrong with being polite?"

When Colby and Cody were safely in my truck and couldn't hear what we were saying, I said, "It's not okay for a stranger to come up and single out a child and speak to him like that. Especially given your history with his mom."

"What history? Man, who the hell are you? *History*."

"Come on, Kevin," Mason said. "Let's go."

There were no other shops around this new ill-fated video store/sub shop/ice cream parlor, and no one else was anywhere around us. The only other people in the vicinity were in slow-moving cars passing by on Main.

"No," he said. "I want to know who's talkin' to me this way about my son."

"He's not your son," I said as if I really knew. "Candace had a paternity test done before she went missing and he's not yours."

"That's good," Mason said. "We want to start a family of our own. Come on, Kevin. Let's go."

"No way he's yours," Kevin said. "So just who the hell're you?"

"I'm just one among a town full of people who are going to find those kids' mom, figure out who took her, and make sure they are protected and cared for."

"He's one of the sheriff's sons," Mason said. "Don't say anything else. Come on, Kevin. Let's go. Now."

"You better hope you don't run into me again," Kevin said to me.

"No need to wait," I said, taking a step toward him. "We're both here now. You can even turn around and take a few steps away and then walk back and run into me again."

Whatever he was on made him mouthy but not brave.

"Yeah, like I'm gonna beat up the sheriff's kid on Main Street."

"Tell you what," I said, "you beat me up and I swear to you no one will hear it from me—not even the sheriff. Your girl over there jumped Candace in the Oasis parking lot and sucker punched her and nothing happened to her."

"Dude," Mason said to me, "Kevin's a lover not a fighter, so if there's any fighting to be done it will be with me."

"That won't work," I said. "I've already seen you. No way you can sneak up and sucker punch me now. Of course, you could wait until I drive away and then try to run me off the road on my way home."

Something flickered in her eyes and she grabbed Kevin by the wrist with one hand, opened Ronnie B's door with the other, and pulled him inside.

"Y'ALL OKAY?" I asked as I climbed into my truck.

They nodded as they continued to eat their ice cream.

"Who was that?" Cody asked.

"One of mom's old boyfriends," Colby said.

"I know people like that can be scary," I said, "and I know right now with your mom missing the whole world's scary in a new way, but . . . I just want you to know that there are several of us that are going to look out for you. Your mom's friends, Lina, Kenny, and Kimmy. Me and my friends, Merrill and Anna. And my dad is the sheriff and he's gonna be looking after you too. I know it doesn't feel like it right now, but you're safe and—"

"Actually," Colby said, "it's the first time we've ever really felt safe."

30

It is the chief paradox of Florida that the south part of the state resembles the north part of the country and the north part of the state resembles the south part of the country.

There are two Floridas.

The one that most people are familiar with, that of Disney and South Beach. The second one that most people drive through or fly over on their way to the first one—the Florida of pickup trucks and gun racks, house trailers with cars on blocks in the yard, the rural Florida of poverty and pine trees.

Pottersville was a part of the second Florida, Gloria Jahoda's *Other Florida*, a rural town much like those of South Georgia and Alabama.

In a place like Pottersville, where there wasn't a lot to do, a Friday night high school football game was a social event. When it was the July jamboree game, it was the social event of the year.

Why football in the summer? It was Pottersville. Every other game was played in the fall but the July jamboree was reserved for the early summer to correspond with the other celebrated annual event—the Pottersville Possum Festival.

When I walked inside the football field gate, Merrill was standing there waiting for me. His clothes matched his skin tone—midnight. He wore black tailored slacks with a thin white pinstripe, black-and-white wing tip shoes, and a black collarless long-sleeve shirt.

People swarmed around everywhere—lining the fence around the field, standing in line at the concession stand, sitting in the bleachers.

Cheerleaders roamed around selling programs and blue and white shakers while the two teams, on opposite ends of the field, warmed up.

In stark contrast to Merrill's cat-burglar ensemble, I wore Levi's 550 stone-washed straight-leg jeans, leather deck shoes with no socks, and a white collarless long-sleeve shirt.

As we approached the home bleachers, Merrill extracted a quarter from his pocket and said, "Call it."

"Tails," I said.

Merrill flipped the coin.

"Tails," he said. "You win. What will it be, eighty or twenty?"

For as long as I could remember, the bleachers had been divided up into eighty-twenty. The first eighty percent, the unofficial white section, the last twenty, the unofficial black section.

"Twenty," I said.

We walked along the narrow sidewalk at the front of the bleachers past the white section, where a few people spoke to us, down to the black section, where a few more people spoke to us.

We sat down beside a heavy black

woman whom everybody called Miss Tanya. She said, "Boys, how y'all doin' tonight?"

"Just fine, Miss Tanya. How are you?" I said.

"Honey," she said, "I am blessed."

When the game started, Miss Tanya yelled, "Come on, Tigers. Kick some butt!" Her whole body, all three hundred pounds, bounced up and down as she yelled.

Miss Tanya continued to talk to us and to the players throughout the first quarter. Merrill and I were quiet—he watching the game, I looking for Laura.

Near the end of the second quarter I spotted her. She was on the other side of the field helping the jamboree court prepare for its halftime program.

I could see that all of the young ladies on the jamboree court and most of the women helping them had on corsages, but Laura did not.

"Idiot!" I exclaimed.

"That *was* stupid," Merrill said. "The whole left side of the field was open."

"No, not that. I forgot something. Miss Tanya," I said looking over at her, "where'd you get that corsage?"

"From the school this afternoon. Shaniqua bought it for me."

"Are they still selling them?"

"I don't think so, baby. What is it?"

"I'm meeting a girl tonight and I forgot to get her one."

"Here," she said and, began to pull the pin out of hers, "take this one, baby."

"No, I couldn't," I said.

"Don't argue with Miss Tanya. Now go on —take it, boy. Go on now. Take it to her."

"Thank you," I said, and gave her a hug. "I'll see you in a little while," I said to Merrill.

"If things don't go well, you'll see me in a little while. If things go well . . ."

"I'll see you Monday."

As I walked over to the visitors' side of the field, I thought about how generous Miss Tanya had been. Every time I wondered why I was living in a place like Pottersville, something like this happened to remind me.

Laura was straightening the corsage on her sister when I reached her. She wore a peach sundress with shoulder straps and light brown sandals. Her summer tanned skin contrasted nicely with the dress and the sandals. Her toenails were painted to match her dress. Her light brown hair, roughly the color of her sandals, was held in a ponytail by a peach bow.

"Prettiest woman here needs a corsage," I whispered when I came up behind her.

She spun around, her brilliant, deep brown eyes twinkling flirtatiously.

"Here?" she said. "Just *here*? Not the county? Or the country?"

As I pinned Miss Tanya's flower on her dress, she said, "Watch your hands there, Priest. Wouldn't want to be an occasion of sin for you."

"More like an occasion of grace," I said.

"How long is this going to take?" she asked. "This your first time? Pinning a corsage on a woman."

"Of course not, but it has been a while."

"I'm sorry I'm giving you such a hard time," she said.

"No you're not."

"Are you finished playing with my breasts yet, Preacher?" she said, her voice louder than it had been.

Before I could respond, Laura's sister

walked back from where she had been gig-
gling with some of her friends.

"This is Father John," Laura said. "The
priest I was telling you about."

"I'm Kim."

"Hey, Kim. I'm John Jordan. And I'm not
a priest."

"I know. She likes you. That's just her obnoxious way of showing it."

"Hey, JJ," Ernie yelled from where he
stood with the rest of the kids waiting to
enter the field.

"Well, I've got to go," Kim said. "Wish me
luck."

"Good luck," I said. "You look great."

LATER THAT NIGHT we danced to Boz Scaggs's
"Look What You've Done to Me."

It reminded me of high school—distant
dances and young love.

"I think your dress is overpowering me."

"Oh yeah? Why's that?" she whispered.

"Because I'd swear you smell like
peaches."

She smiled.

Still later that night, I took her home and kissed her good night.

It was a perfect first kiss. Gentle, slightly lingering, hinting of more, much more.

31

L aura and I were headed to Tallahassee beneath a bank of gray rain clouds.

Thunder rumbled in the distance.

We were on Highway 20 in Dad's new Ford Explorer—borrowed because my old Chevy S-10 was too rough a ride for a day date to Tallahassee.

Laura, who was far less talkative today, looked regal in her long, fitted black dress. Hair down, small gold loop earrings, a single gold chain around her neck. Understated. Devastating.

"When are you going to tell me why we're dressed like this?" she asked.

I was wearing a black Mark Alexander suit with a gray pinstripe, a black shirt with an Episcopal collar, and black wing tip shoes.

"Did you bring a change of clothes?" I asked.

"Yes, but that doesn't answer my question."

So far I had learned that she is working at FedEx while finishing up her master's degree in counseling at FSU. She and her dad live in Tallahassee, though not together, her mom and sister in Pottersville, where she visits most weekends. Her mom teaches school and is the sister of the wealthy Pottersville bank president, and her sister Kim plans to attend TCC in the fall.

"You don't like surprises?" I asked.

"No. Not really."

I nodded. "We are going out to eat and to listen to jazz in the park and to spend a leisurely afternoon in our state's beautiful capital after the funeral of an inmate who was killed on Monday."

"You're taking me to a funeral on our first date? I hate funerals."

"Don't know anybody who loves them."

The sides of the highway, like every highway in rural Northwest Florida, were lined with rows and rows of slash pines. Occasionally, when the sun peeked out from the gathering rain clouds, it shone just above and behind the rows of trees, causing them to cast shadows across the highway that looked like prison bars.

"I arranged for you to stay with some friends of mine during the funeral if you don't want to go. Or I could drop you at the mall. It'll take less than an hour."

"You go to a lot of inmates' funerals?" she said.

"This is my first," I said. "But I'm new."

"Why this one?" she asked.

"His family asked me to do it."

"You're *doing* the funeral?" she asked, her eyes widening.

I nodded.

"Did you know the family from before?" she asked.

"I've never met them, and if I met the inmate, I don't remember it."

She was quiet a moment, and I could tell she was processing all this.

"You've been giving me such a hard

time I thought it'd be funny to surprise you with a funeral, but you don't have to go."

The sun peeked out from behind the clouds and reflected off the car in front of us. I put on my shades.

When I pulled out into the other lane to pass, I noticed Laura reached over and grabbed the door handle, her knuckles turning red then white.

After we had safely passed the car and she had time to recuperate, she said, "If we make it to Tallahassee, I'd like to go to the funeral with you."

The clouds covered the sun again. I pulled my shades off.

"Now will you tell me about yourself?" I asked.

"I don't know. You seem to see way too much as it is."

I looked at her with an expression that said *I don't buy it.*

THE FUNERAL HOME was actually a small double-wide trailer only slightly larger than mine, but plenty big enough for the small number of people who showed up for Ike Johnson's funeral.

In addition to Laura and myself, there were four other people there—two elderly black ladies, his grandma and aunt, and two young people, his sister and his friend.

The funeral home was named Jack's. It didn't even say Jack's Funeral Home on the sign—just Jack's.

An uneven number of wooden pews sat on the thin red carpet that smelled like feet and old socks.

I had wrestled with what to say all week. I felt it must be something about love's ability to redeem the worst of situations and people, but until I began to speak, I didn't know exactly what I would say.

"According to one of my favorite passages from the Hebrew Bible, God's mercies are new every morning. Every single morning, God's infinite mercies are fresh and unused and waiting for us. They were waiting for Ike this morning no less than for you and me. You may say that Ike didn't live the way he should have and so surely God's mercies were not available for him. But I say that it is exactly when we don't do what we should that we need mercy most, and it is also when mercy is most available to us.

"Grace is not what we deserve, but what we need. Justice gives us what we deserve, but grace gives us what we need. If God doesn't love Ike as much as he does you and me, then God's love is conditional. But if love is perfect, if God is love, then we are all loved beyond reason, beyond deserving, beyond understanding.

"Today, like every day, all we have to do is accept the absolute, unconditional, perfect love of God—accept it and let ourselves be changed by it. As for Ike, remember Jesus's parable of the prodigal son—welcomed home even after he rejected his dad, ran away to a foreign land, wasted all his money on parties and prostitutes. No matter what we do, we are wanted, we are welcome to come home.

"This past Tuesday, Ike closed his eyes in this world and opened them in the next. I trust he opened them to the familiar and loving eyes of a father, who welcomed him home. Jonathan Edwards, the famous Puritan preacher, was wrong. We're not sinners in the hands of an angry God. We're sinners in the hands of a merciful and loving God."

After the funeral, the family thanked me and tried to pay me but I wouldn't take it.

As Laura and I were preparing to leave, the young man said to be a friend of Ike's asked if he could talk to me.

"I loved Ike," he said, looking down at the floor. "I even went to see him a couple of times in prison. But then something happened to him. Drugs, I think, but something else too. He got in over his head. I think they killed him. I wanted you to know."

"Who do you think killed him?" I asked.

"Whoever he was involved with," he said.

"What's your name?" I asked.

"Don Hall."

"Is there a number I can reach you at if I find something out or need to ask you more questions?"

He shook his head and walked away. After taking about five steps, he stopped, nearly turned around, but then continued walking.

"Do you believe all that?" Laura asked when we were back in the car.

"Believe all what?" I asked.

"All those things you said in your message, which was excellent and perfectly appropriate, by the way."

"Thank you. Yes, I do."

"How can you believe such things when the world is the way it is?"

"How can I not?"

"You spoke about mercy and grace, but where is it really? Where do you see any evidence of it? I really want to know."

"Dancing with you last night. That was a grace. And your peach perfume. A good book. Sunset. Sunrise. A rainy night. The love of a parent. The loyalty of a friend. Grace surrounds us."

"But you can't know all of this, that all those things have meaning?"

"I get that it's all wishful thinking, hope and faith, but . . . they have meaning to me."

32

U nder cover of a small oak grove, I parked on an old twin-path logging road in Dad's Explorer.

I had taken Laura home after our day in Tallahassee, and was parked in a location that gave me a good view of the prison without being observed by Tower One.

If I had been observed, the roving patrol would have driven out to investigate. If an officer had driven out, I would have been in trouble in more ways than one.

There was, I just discovered while searching for a flashlight, a firearm in the vehicle. Firearms on state prison property were against the law.

In addition to the Smith .38, Dad had an expensive pair of binoculars, which came in handy.

I sat there in the dark watching and thinking, my window rolled down.

Eventually Captain Skipper appeared near the front of the institution—walking an inmate into the sally port and getting into a van.

In violation of DOC policy, the inmate was neither cuffed nor shackled, and there was no armed officer accompanying them.

The front gate rolled open and the van pulled out of the institution, heading down the two-mile county road to the main highway into town.

I followed.

The night was pleasant, the moon full, the sky clear.

I followed a quarter of a mile back with my lights off.

When the van reached the main highway, it turned toward town.

As I neared the intersection, a car passed by on the main highway. Turning my lights on, I followed it, leaving it between me and the van.

At the next intersection, some two miles from town, the van turned left and the car between us continued straight.

When the van had a sufficient lead again, I turned and followed.

The highway was desolate, with only the occasional house or trailer, most of which sat a good distance off the road under the cover of pine trees.

Pulling over and using the binoculars, I gave the van as much of a lead as possible.

About a mile and a half up on the right, the van turned in to the residence of Russ Maddox, the president of Potter State Bank, the wealthiest man in Potter County and Laura's uncle.

Russ Maddox was a middle-aged bachelor who had lived alone for as long as I could remember. Slightly effeminate, odd and awkward, he was the subject of much small-town speculation.

By the time I reached the driveway, the van had disappeared into the woods that served as Russ's front yard.

I pulled the Explorer off the road about a half mile down from the driveway and moved through the woods toward what was known in town as Maddox Mansion.

The light from the moon shone down so brightly the pines cast shadows.

No breeze. No movement.

The undergrowth was thick, moving through it slow, and at one point I tripped over a fallen scrub oak it was camouflaging.

The ground was dew damp and cooler than I expected.

When I reached the end of the woods at the edge of the yard, I could see the front of the house.

The house was dark, the only illumination visible coming from a security light near the closed garage doors. In front of them I could see Maddox's dusty-rose-colored Lincoln and a gray Toyota Tercel.

Skipper was banging on the imposing solid oak door, the inmate beside him. I couldn't be positive from this distance, but something about the inmate reminded me of Anthony Thomas.

After a few more minutes of banging, Skipper and the inmate turned to leave. When they did, I saw that it was Anthony Thomas. He was walking like he was drunk.

Skipper helped him into the van and then jumped in himself. In another few moments they were gone.

My watch read 1:46 a.m. as I ran toward the Explorer.

It took me three minutes to reach the Explorer—far longer than Skipper needed to reach the end of the driveway.

I paused at the edge of the woods to see which way the van would turn, but it was already gone.

33

On Sunday morning, beneath a clear blue sky and sunny, hot day, I drove out to Dad's secluded little five-acre farm to return his vehicle.

"Thanks for the use of the Explorer," I said.

"How'd the date go? Come in for a minute. I need to talk to you."

He led me down the short hallway to a great room with very little furniture in it. A large stacked-stone fireplace on the back wall had an unvarnished wood hearth that was filled with pictures and marksman trophies. Above the fireplace on the dark paneled wall, the head of a large elk was mounted.

He took a seat in an old gray recliner that was positioned in front of the TV. It creaked when he plopped down in it. The only other place to sit was a dark gray couch in front of the wall opposite the fireplace, but to sit there was to sit behind him, so I stood.

The house smelled as it always smelled —dusty, slightly mildewed, and like a pack of wild dogs lived there. The pack-of-wild-dogs smell came from Wallace, an Irish setter who was currently occupying the couch—another reason I stood.

Before he got to what he needed to talk to me about, I told him about what I had seen at Russ Maddox's house last night—an account I had already given twice this morning, once to Daniels and once to Stone.

We talked about Ike Johnson's death and the investigation and what Molly Thomas had told me and what else Skipper might be up to, but it didn't amount to much more than me just keeping him informed about what was going on in the county where he was the chief law enforcement officer.

"What'd you need to talk to me about?" I said.

"It's about your mother," he said.

They divorced when I was fourteen, when her drinking had progressed to the point that it was no longer safe to leave my brother and me with her. He divorced her after almost eighteen years and about a million second chances. It was at this time that my sister Nancy divorced herself from our entire family and moved to Chicago.

"She's . . . I spoke to her doctor. She has cirrhosis of the liver and kidney failure. Doesn't have long."

"You sure? She called me the other night drunk."

"It's her medication. She's in the hospital. Makes her sound drunk."

I thought about how I had spoken to her, guilt spreading through me.

"She needs someone right now," Dad said, "and that can't be me. Jake's not cut out for it, and the only thing Nancy's going to do is dance when she's dead. It can only be you. It's got to be you."

· · ·

"I KNOW of no other way to put this," I said.

"Okay," Jasper Evans said.

He was a huge man—one of the largest inmates on the compound. Well over six and a half feet tall, well over three hundred pounds, with skin the color of Tupelo honey and teeth to match.

"I hear you're one of the main suppliers of drugs on the compound."

We were seated in my office in the chapel.

It was less than an hour until the worship service and the sounds of the choir rehearsing could be heard from within the chapel sanctuary. They were working on the song for today's service, "Power in the Blood"—a song I had never cared for.

Since he didn't respond, I said, "Is it true?"

He shrugged, tilted his head, and made a *What can I say?* expression.

"How long you been dealing?"

"Don't deal. Supply."

"You can no longer be our choir director."

"Why? It's two different things. I know

doing that shit ain't right. I don't do it. I just transport a little of it—and not any of the hard stuff. But I love to sing. 'Specially Gospel music."

"I know you do. And you're good at it. But I can't let you lead the choir."

"I got to sing," he said.

I nodded. "But not in the choir and not as the choir director."

"You our chaplain because you perfect?"

I shook my head. "You don't have to be perfect. But you can't be a drug dealer."

"This because of what happened to Ike. Had nothing to do with that."

"Who did?"

He shrugged. "He was taken care of. That's who did him. Wasn't no inmate. Had to be an officer. He do whatever the hell he want. Get high every day. Stopped getting it from me a long time ago."

I nodded. "Thanks for the info. See you at the service in a little while."

"Not if I ain't singing you won't."

AFTER THE SERVICE, I went down to Medical.

I knew the body had been hidden in the

closet there. I knew that Johnson, Jacobson, and Thomas all spent a great deal of time there and were all involved in whatever was going on.

"Hey, Chaplain," Nurse Anderson greeted me loudly as I approached the medical building. She was standing outside smoking.

She was a large, attractive woman with bleached-blond hair, green eyes the color of lime Jell-O, and bright red lips.

"How's it going?"

"Just fine. You?"

Smoke came out of her mouth as she talked, and when she wasn't speaking, she was puffing. In contrast to the dainty Capris that Sandy Strickland smoked, Anderson smoked full-sized Winstons. She held the pack along with a lighter and a paper cup with large red lipstick stains on it in her left hand.

"Anyone in the infirmary today?"

She nodded. "Two lucky winners."

Behind us a steady stream of inmates, returning from the chapel, library, or dining hall, made their way back to the dorms. A couple of them remarked on my message as they went by. Many of them spoke or waved to Nurse Anderson. She was warm and friendly to all of them.

"Infirmary's a pretty popular place, isn't it?" I asked.

"You have no idea," she said with a wink. "A lot of these men just need some female TLC."

"ATTENTION ON THE COMPOUND," a loud voice said over the PA system. The words echoed off the buildings. "RECALL. INMATES RETURN TO YOUR DORM. RE-CALL. INMATES RETURN TO YOUR DORM." The stream of inmates behind us became a rushing river of blue.

"Aren't you usually on the night shift?" I asked.

"We're all working overtime to prepare for the ACA inspection," she said. "I work midnights mostly."

I nodded and she took a long drag on her cigarette and a big gulp of her coffee.

"Wasn't that just awful what happened to poor little Ike Johnson?" she said. "He was here the night before it happened. I talked with him for a pretty good while. We weren't that busy. I just can't believe it. Really freaked me out."

"Who was in the infirmary that night with him?" I asked.

She thought for a minute. "Let me see," she said, "seems like it was only Thomas, Jacobson, and Johnson. I think that's right. We usually have more than that, so it sort of stands out, you know? Especially after what happened."

"Anthony Thomas?" I asked.

She nodded.

"I saw him in Confinement a couple of days ago and he was on something strong. Didn't seem like the side effects of something prescribed. Officer down there said to ask you what he's on."

"Nothing as far as I know," she said. "I'd have to look at his chart to be sure, but . . . Probably got his hands on something illegal. Such a shame. What a waste."

"And you're sure he was there that night?"

"I believe so. He's there a lot. I don't think there was anyone else that night. Come on, let's go back there and take a look at the log, then I can tell you for sure."

"Sure," I said. "Thanks."

She led me inside to the nurses' station and began flipping through the pages of the log book.

"Just Johnson and Jacobson according to this," she said, "but I know Thomas was here. I remember. Oh well, somebody just forgot to write it down."

"*Somebody forgot to write it down?*" I asked, my voice revealing my incredulity.

"I know. It shouldn't have happened. Usually doesn't. Anyway, I know he was here. Saw him with my own two baby blues."

"Blues?" I asked.

"Oh," she said smiling. "Yeah. I have colored contacts on."

"So Johnson, Jacobson, and Thomas were the only ones here last Monday night, right?"

"Right. I'm sure of it."

"Who took the trash out that morning?" I asked.

She gave me a large shrug. "That's the sixty-four-thousand-dollar question, isn't it?" She leaned in closer to me and whispered, "I can tell you who it wasn't. It wasn't Jones. He was cleaning up a urine sample for me. I saw the bags when I went and got him, and when we went back, they were gone. Oh, and it wasn't me. I was with Jones the whole time. So the two of us are in the clear."

"Unless," I said, "you did it together."

34

"She wasn't being abused per se," Wendy Hollister was saying of Candace Miles, "at least not physically, but she did feel trapped, like she really couldn't make a clean break and like she was about to be pulled back into certain . . . activities and, ah, practices . . . that she didn't want to return to. We're not just a shelter for battered women. We're a refuge for any woman in need."

Hope House was located at the West End of Panama City Beach near Highway 79. As expected, it didn't look like what it was. Its exterior had the appearance of a self-storage facility complete with a chain-link fence around it and an armed guard at the gate.

Wendy Hollister, the tired, middle-aged, schoolmarm-looking platinum blonde with too much makeup who ran the place, met us up front in the reception and refused to let us go anywhere else on the premises.

"Is she here now?" I asked.

She shook her head. "No, I'm—"

"Was she?" I asked. "Has she been?"

"If you'll let me finish I'll tell you," she said. "One question at a time. Please. No. She never showed."

"But she planned to come?" I asked.

"Yes, absolutely."

"Did she plan to bring her children?"

"Yes, of course, but not right away. They were to have joined her a few days later. We have a process in place that ensures the safety and privacy of everyone involved."

"What's that?" I asked.

"The mother comes first, then a few days later the children are taken by the state, but instead of placing them in foster care they bring them here. It's really ingenious."

"And that's what she was going to do but never did?" I asked.

"Exactly. A friend of hers was going to help her get away, then notify the authorities which would trigger having her children picked up, and we'd get them after that. But none of that happened because she never showed."

I said, "When was she supposed to have arrived?"

"The night she went missing," she said. "We just thought she changed her mind, lost her nerve. It happens a lot. But then a day or two after, we saw on the news where she had disappeared."

"And you don't have any idea where she is?" I asked.

"Absolutely none."

"Did she mention any other plans— somewhere she might go instead?"

"Not to me."

"Was she afraid of anyone?" I asked. "Besides her boyfriend, I mean. Was there anyone who was trying to stop her from leaving or—"

"She wasn't afraid of her boyfriend," she said. "At least not in the way you mean. She was afraid of never being able to leave him, of getting back on drugs to deal with his codependency and excessive neediness, but not of him hurting her physically. I think one of the regulars at the bar where she worked creeped her out, but I didn't get the sense that he scared her. The only person she was truly afraid of was her dealer—or ex-dealer. He truly frightened her and I'd say she was coming here to get away from him as much or more than Steve."

35

Big Baby Bear was an enormous black guy who was always smiling. He was always accompanied by Boogie Bowers, a tall, thin mixed-race man who never smiled.

Bear was responsible for nearly ninety percent of the drug trade in Pottersville, Boogie for nearly all its casualties.

Merrill and I found the two men fishing with cane poles from the banks at Potter Landing, the sun gleaming off Bear's big bald head.

"Merrill Monroe and John fuckin' Jordan," Bear said as we walked up. Whacha'll doin' up out here? Ain't to wet your worms, ain't carrying no poles."

"Maybe we came to see how it done first," Merrill said. "'Fo' we try it ourselves."

Merrill, who often slipped in and out of Ebonics and formal register on a whim, was never as straight-up street as when dealing with people like Bear and Boogie.

"Then nigga, you come to the right place," Bear said, "'cause Papa Bear know how to pulls 'em in. Hell, I could pay some-body to do this for me, but I love this shit. And I'm got-damn good at it."

"The best," Boogie said without looking up.

"Boogie, what the hell you know about it?" Bear said. "Nigga can't catch a fish fo' shit. Only time I ever seen him catch a mess enough for dinner was in shallow water, and this nigga drew his gat out and shot the bitches."

"Caught 'em though, didn't I?" Boogie said.

"*Shee-it*," Bear said, "wasn't enough left of 'em to eat. Little bit that was would give you lead poison."

Merrill and I waited while the two men

reminisced about that time Boogie shot all them fish.

Eventually Bear said, "Whatcha'll really here for, 'cause I know it ain't for no damn fishin' lesson."

"Came to ask you about that white woman that went missin'," Merrill said. "Candace Miles."

"Y'all think Big Bear got her back at his den?" he said.

"No, just lookin' for a little 4-1-1 help us find her," Merrill said.

"She's got two kids," I said. "Trying to help 'em get their mama back."

"Why?" Bear asked. "I's a kid when my moms split and look how good I growed up to be."

"That's true," Merrill said, "but these white youngins ain't as tough or resourceful as Big Bear."

"Truth," Bear said.

We are all quiet for a moment.

"I ain't yanked that pale bitch," Bear said. "Got no idea who did. She and I did a little business back in the day, but that's been some time, and it was always just business. Tried to slip the dick to her back then but she only wanted the shit. Big Bear got plenty of little mama bears wantin' to give him all the sweet honey he can handle, so it was nothin' but a thang."

"Mind lettin' us know, you hear anything?" Merrill said.

"Nah, man, I don't mind. I'll ask around see what I can find out. Shee-it, who knows? Big Bear find her ass and reunite her with her little cubs, maybe she come off a little of that white girl trim."

36

"You been drinkin'?" Jake asked.

I had just arrived at Russ Maddox's house, which was now a crime scene.

Jake Jordan and I were brothers. So were Cain and Abel.

He had been waiting for me in the driveway, chest out, arms dangling wide of his body to accommodate his muscles and gun.

Two years my junior, he also had brown eyes and light brown hair, and although we were both roughly six feet tall, he outweighed me by almost fifty pounds. His dark green deputy sheriff's uniform shirt was at least two sizes too small, and his pants puckered and pulled at the pleats.

"I don't think you should be here at all, but no way I'm lettin' you through if you been drinkin'."

I continued past him. "Where's Dad?"

"Inside," he said, turning to walk with me.

When Jake and I were growing up, we both competed for the approval of our childhood hero, our dad. We both received Dad's approval, but I had received more and was more like a friend than a son. Jake hated me for it.

When I moved to Atlanta after high school, Jake moved into the top spot, even eventually becoming one of Dad's deputies. When I abandoned law enforcement for ministry, my relationship with Dad was strained even further. But since I'd been back, Jake's insecurities had kicked into overdrive.

"Looks like Russ was murdered," he said. "Pretty damn exciting. Two years without a homicide where we didn't know exactly who did it, and now we have two in a week."

I nodded.

"When're you going to see Mom?" he asked.

"Soon," I said. "Soon as I can. Next day or so. You?"

He shook his head. "I just can't deal with that kind of shit. Probably ride over when Dad goes. Next weekend maybe."

"Nancy know?" I asked.

"Dad said he was going to call her tomorrow, but I told him he shouldn't. Hell, she ain't even a part of this family anymore."

JACK JORDAN, looking tired and older than he should have, spoke with the medical examiner in hushed and quiet tones.

The body of Russ Maddox was slumped over in an uncomfortable-looking wingback chair covered in plastic and positioned in front of the television. Like the chair, the entire house looked uncomfortable. If it were lived in, you couldn't tell it.

"John," Dad said when he saw me.

"Dad." I nodded.

I walked over to the chair where Russ's obese body sat crumpled. His head hung down, the fat gathering beneath his third chin and in large rolls of white blubber around his midsection. He was wearing a white silk robe, which gaped open revealing white silk boxer shorts and a tight white silk T-shirt.

Beside his chair stood an ornately carved wooden TV tray with an open bottle of wine, a wineglass, and a small china plate with caviar and crackers on it.

My eyes widened when I noticed the two long, sharp kitchen knives lying near the plate. The knives seemed to be spaced too far apart from the plate, and they were positioned funny. It was just an impression, but it looked as if they had been added later. I looked back at Maddox. There was no sign of violence or trauma anywhere on his body. In stark contrast to the last death I had witnessed, there was not a single drop of blood.

"That *is* caviar, isn't it?" I asked.

"Yes, it is," the medical examiner said.

"Is it generally eaten with large carving knives?"

"Curious, isn't it?" he asked.

"You ever been accused of exaggeration, Roger?" I asked.

He smiled, but did not comment.

I looked over at Dad. He just shrugged.

"Any prints?" I asked.

"On the bottle, the glass, the plate, the tray—everything but the knives. They're clean," Dad said.

"I did find small traces of the light powder residue that is usually associated with surgical latex gloves," Roger stated as if he had said that he had found wine in the wine bottle.

"Well, now," I said. "Okay for me to look around?"

"Everything's been dusted, if that's what you mean," Jake responded. He took a tooth-pick out of his mouth and tucked it into the left breast pocket of his deputy's shirt.

"Take a look," Dad said, and then gave Jake a look that said *back off*.

I walked across the sculpted Berber car-pet, which covered the entire house save the mahogany floors in the kitchen, dining, and foyer areas.

In the kitchen, brass pots, colanders, and ladles hung over a butcher-block island. Like the counters, there was nothing on it, and it had been cleaned to the point of shining. Expensive wineglasses were suspended under the glassed cabinet housing his fine china.

I walked out of the spotless kitchen into the formal living room. Every single piece of upholstered furniture sported carefully placed afghans, as if being preserved for an event yet to come. Every piece of wooden furniture was fitted with a sheet of custom-cut glass to cover the top.

With the exception of the dead body in the living room, the entire house could have been a fine furniture store showroom.

Evidently the crime-scene investigation was nearly concluded when I had been called. The house was virtually empty. I did, however, pass by a young female deputy as I was walking up the stairs, but she didn't seem to be investigating.

I smiled and nodded at her. She didn't return either gesture.

She obviously felt the need to establish her seriousness as a law enforcement officer at a crime scene.

I was convinced.

The second story of the house was as im-maculate as the first—nothing out of place and no sign that human beings actually resided here.

Every hallway had a long plastic runner covering the carpet, making my shoes sound like small circular saws as I shuffled along them.

There were three bedrooms—and if someone had ever spent a single night in any of them, I couldn't tell it.

The one I assumed was Russ's, because of its size and attached bathroom, was nearly two times the size of my trailer. The bed, a king-size monstrosity, was at least four feet off the floor with massive spiral posts at each corner and looked to be mahogany. The other furniture in the room seemed to be an eclectic gathering of priceless antiques gleaned from different parts of the world—an armoire, tallboy, full-length free-standing mirror, vanity, and dresser.

The walk-in closet was neatly organized. The back wall was covered with shoe bins from floor to ceiling, each containing a pair of polished shoes. Each side of the closet had a rack with clothes hanging on it, suits and dress shirts mainly. I looked around the closet and the bedroom and found nothing unusual.

The bathroom was another matter.

Under the expensive porcelain sink with gold and brass fittings, there were three large jars of Vaseline, four tubes of K-Y lubrication jelly, and two large boxes of condoms.

The other two bedrooms were a lot like the larger one, only smaller. They were showroom-clean and decorated like ones seen in magazines. I made what I thought was a pretty thorough search of the rooms and then went back into the master suite.

Looking through Russ's drawers was like shopping at Macy's. Everything looked new, and there were several packages of under-wear and socks and T-shirts that had never been opened.

I walked over and looked under the bed. It was spotless.

I was tempted to believe Russ Maddox might be a little on the obsessive-compulsive side, but I knew the dangers of rushing to judgement.

After finding nothing on the back side of the headboard and the mirror, I opened the two doors of the armoire, exposing a 32-inch television, VCR, and camcorder.

Beneath the shelf under the TV and VCR, there were several videotapes— movies ranging from *The Sound of Music* to *Rocky*.

I pulled a few of the tapes out of the boxes and popped a few of them into the VCR. They were what they appeared to be.

As I started to replace them, I noticed that behind them, lying on their sides, were four of the oversized Disney VHS boxes —*Bambi*, *Dumbo*, *Beauty and the Beast*, and *The Lion King*. I stood them up vertically alongside the other tapes and closed the armoire doors.

I started to leave the room, and then it hit me. Why would somebody as obsessive-compulsive as Maddox lay the Disney tapes horizontally behind the others?

At first I had figured it was just because they were too tall to fit, but putting them back like the others disproved that. It also proved that there was room for them.

And why would a single, middle-aged man like Russ Maddox have Disney movies anyway?

I went back and opened the doors again and then the Disney boxes.

The labels on the tapes corresponded with the boxes, but they were typed home-made labels and not the printed labels that usually were affixed to tapes in the dubbing houses. Homemade labels would have made sense if the tapes were copied, but if they were copies they wouldn't be in the Disney boxes.

I placed one in the VCR. The TV screen blinked from royal blue to a shot of two men having sex on the bed in the very room I was standing in. The camera seemed to be shooting the video footage from where it still sat on the shelf beside the VCR. The room was well lit, and the camera was obviously an expensive one because the picture was crystal clear. It showed a fat white man from the side hunched over a thin black man. The fat white man was Russ Maddox. He was moaning and occasionally blurting out ob-scenities. The other man, whose face I could not see, was making noises too, but his seemed to be more pain than pleasure.

In another minute or so, Russ had cli-maxed and collapsed, the black man disappearing beneath his blubber. I hit the fast forward button on the machine, and in a few seconds the black man beneath Russ began moving slightly and Russ finally rolled off him. The black man jumped up. When he did, he came face-to-face with the eye of the camera. I paused it on the familiar face of Ike Johnson.

I stopped the tape as I heard a voice from the hall.

"John, your dad would like to see you downstairs," the serious young female officer said when she reached the door to the bedroom.

"Would you mind asking him to step up here? I need to show him something."

A few moments later Dad and Jake stepped into the room.

"Body's gone," Dad said. "Crime scene is gone. We're about to go. Just wanted to touch base with you, see if you thought your case and this one are related."

"Yeah, I'm pretty sure they are," I said, and pressed Play on the VCR.

Jake said, "Just threw up in my mouth some."

"Who's that with Russ?" Dad asked.

"The inmate who was killed on Tuesday," I said. "Ike Johnson."

He nods and frowns. "Looks like maybe Russ was poisoned. Seems completely opposite to how your guy was killed—as opposite as you can get. We really thinking the same doer did both?"

I shrugged. "Not sure about that. Just that they're connected. Though they may not be as different as they seem."

"How so?"

"If both were drugged—and if the killer isn't the trash officer who stabbed Ike—then all the killer did was drug him and put him in the bag, making his part of it as bloodless as this one."

37

"I think Captain Skipper has been supplying inmate prostitutes to Russ Maddox. And Ike Johnson was one of them," I said.

I was sitting with Merrill and Anna in her office on the morning of the longest Monday of my life, a day that I began in the company of my friends and ended in the hands of my enemies.

"Run that by me one more time," Anna said.

"You heard me. And the two people who've died recently both have ties to Skipper and each other."

"What do you mean?" Anna asked.

I told them.

When I finished, they were both silent.

I could see the wheels turning in Anna's head. I knew that wheels were also turning in Merrill's head, but I couldn't see them.

"It's just not possible," Anna said at last. "There's no way he could pull it off. It would take . . ."

"Help from higher up," Merrill said.

I shrugged. "It's a possibility."

"At least," Anna added. "But he couldn't do it without getting caught."

"He has been," Merrill said. "John caught his ass."

"We've got to call FDLE in," Anna said.

"Daniels says he's going to," I said. "Dad too."

Merrill said, "You saw Johnson on the tape. See anybody else?"

"He's the only one I saw, and it was very short. My guess is Russ wasn't known for his stamina. Dad took the tapes into custody, but I plan to watch them if you wanna help."

"I'm busy that night," Merrill said.

I WENT BACK to my office and ordered flowers

for Laura. I had them write on the card, *The scent of peaches still lingers.*

Next, I called her to see how she and the family were doing.

"Hello."

"Laura?" I said.

"No, this is Kim. Who's this?"

"John Jordan. How are you?"

"I'm fine. Thanks. Let me grab Laura. She's dying to talk to you. She's totally spazzing out over you."

In a moment, Laura picked up.

"Hey, you."

"Morning. How are you?"

"I'm okay. Having contradictory feelings. Coming off the high of a wonderful weekend with you and then the shock of Uncle Russ's death."

"How's your mom?"

"She's okay. They weren't very close. He was so weird. He was not really close to anyone that I know of. Still, it's a shock."

"Anything I can do?"

"Could you come by after work?"

"Sure."

A few moments after I hung up, Mr.

Smith brought an inmate pass in and laid it on my desk.

"Think you might want to talk with this inmate. Need to hear what he has to say."

"Send him in."

Jefferson Hunter rushed into my office. I motioned for him to have a seat.

"When my mother passed, you really helped me a lot," he said. "I remember that. So I had to tell you. Chaplain, you in danger."

"Oh yeah?"

"They's this dude what handles things for people on the 'pound. I ain't gonna say his name, but I want you to know he come up to a small group of some real badasses, you know. He say he got lotsa money for a hit. He say it's protection on the 'pound and about three hundred in canteen. I never heard anyone offer that much for anything. Then he say who he want hit. It you."

I was silent. I couldn't believe it.

"It really surprise me, you know, 'cause you the most popular chaplain we ever had. Everybody on the 'pound say you really care and shit. So when he say he want a hit on you,

I just really couldn't believe it. I thought you should know. But I mean, I ain't no squealer or nothin'. I just doin' you a solid like you done for me when my moms was dying. So we straight, and you didn't hear it from me."

I nodded. "Thank you."

"Just stay off the 'pound awhile, and watch your back."

38

"We know for sure now that Johnson was murdered," Tom Daniels was saying. "He was put to sleep in the early morning hours last Tuesday. We know that his body was kept in the caustic storage closet. The lab tested the cleaner and some fibers that were found on the floor in there and made a match. We think he was drugged between six and seven."

We were back in Stone's office on Monday afternoon giving him an update.

I had been operating under the assumption that Ike had been murdered but now it was confirmed by the lab.

I thought about the timing. If the estimate was right, he was put to sleep just before Security shift change and just after Medical shift change. The two are on slightly different schedules.

"A large quantity of sleeping pills were found hidden in Jacobson's property this weekend," Stone said. "He's been saving them up, not taking them. He's in Confinement now but he was there with Johnson the night he was killed."

"Who found them?" I asked. "Who did the search?"

"Captain Skipper."

"Of course he did," I said. "These pills weren't found when Jacobson's property was searched when he was sent to Confinement, but conveniently as we're gathering evidence against Skipper. Why is he still working? Surely after Saturday night you can suspend him now."

"I'm working on it," Daniels said. "Takes time to build a case. Trying not to tip him off while we investigate him. We're gonna get him—for whatever he's been doing. We just want to get it right—and find out exactly what he's been up to. He may very well have been up to all sorts of corrupt shit but not be guilty of killing anyone. You yourself said he didn't go into Russ Maddox's house around the time he was murdered. This kind of work takes patience. Perhaps you don't have the temperament for it."

I nodded. "I'm sure that's it."

"We don't know for sure Russ Maddox was murdered, do we?" Stone said. "I thought it was possible he died of natural causes."

"It's true there were no obvious signs of foul play," I said, "but . . . I'll be shocked if he wasn't poisoned and if it doesn't have something to do with what happened to Ike."

"And it might, but we can't do anything until we have evidence," Daniels said.

"I talked to the chaplain at Calhoun Correctional about Shutt," I said. "He worked there before transferring here. He said he got nothing but complaints about Shutt—"

"Yeah, but—" Stone interrupted.

"—from staff as well as inmates," I continued.

"Okay," Stone said. "We'll watch him very closely. Anything else?"

"Got the results back on the tests the

FDLE lab did on the carpet in the back of the chapel," Daniels said. "Found small traces of blood and semen. Which means someone has been having sex on the floor in there."

"Confirms Molly Thomas's story," I said.

"Lab also found traces of vaginal fluid."

Stone shook his head and frowned deeply.

As I WALKED into the chapel I could hear my phone ringing. The quick double rings let me know it was an outside call. Unlocking my office door, I rushed over and answered it.

"Dad wanted you to know that it looks like it *was* murder," Jake said when I answered. "Russ Maddox's preliminary autopsy results are back. Looks like he was poisoned. They won't be one-hundred-percent certain until the labs come back, but they found traces of poison in the wine and caviar and there was plenty of both in his stomach."

"Do they have any idea what was used?"

"Not with certainty yet. Chloral hydrate is a front-runner."

"How about a time of death?" I asked.

"ME guesses between 12:30 and 1:30 a.m.," he said. "Russ ate at Rudy's earlier, so he's basing it on that and the stomach contents."

"We shouldn't rule out that it could be Rudy's food that killed him."

"Oh and we got Russ's medical records. Faggot had AIDS. Just like you."

That was Jake's attempt at humor or stupid brotherly banter, but it brought back the fact that I might be infected, a thought I had been working to keep at bay.

39

As I approached the medical building, I could see Nurse Julie Anderson out front smoking again. It seemed at times that was all she did. She perked up when she saw me coming.

"Hey, Chaplain, come here," she said.

Her loud voice changed and she began to whisper, which was roughly the volume most people use in ordinary conversation.

"I really felt bad yesterday about our log book not being right so checked into it. I called the sarge who'd been at the center gate at the time to see if he could remember who went through on their way to Medical that night, and guess what, he did. He said that Thomas didn't come through the gate but that he did go to Medical that night—just from the other side of the compound."

"Did he remember anyone else going in or out?"

"Yeah, he did. I didn't ask him or anything, but he said that later, after my shift was over, he let another inmate through the gate to go to Medical, but that he came back in just a few minutes and said he couldn't find anybody, and, anyway, he didn't want to be charged the three dollars."

Because of all of the abuse of the medical facilities by inmates who just wanted to get out of the sun or see a pretty nurse, the department had instituted a policy that made inmates pay three dollars to the department if they declared a medical emergency and they really didn't have one.

"He say who it was?" I asked.

"Couldn't remember," she said.

"Thank you. I sure appreciate it."

"You're welcome. I'm just sorry somebody was so careless. You going to say anything to anybody about it?"

"No, don't worry. I'd like to talk with Nurse Strickland though. What time does she come in tonight?"

"You're in luck. We're both pulling a double. So she's here today."

I walked through the waiting room, where twenty-five inmates were staring at the wall in front of them in silence. A few of them whispered greetings to me. A couple asked to see me later in the day. I entered the door on the right, which led to the exam rooms and the infirmary.

Strickland was not in any of the exam rooms, nor the nurses' station, nor the infirmary. She was seated in the break room at the end of the hall talking with someone I couldn't see.

When I reached the break room door, inmate Jones walked through it and left without speaking.

"I wondered if I might ask you a couple more questions?" I said.

She looked at her watch. "Sure. They about your tests? You wanna go to my office? How are you feeling?"

"They're about the night before Johnson was killed."

"Someone said they heard you were conducting an investigation. Is that true? Are you not really a chaplain?"

"I'm just helping the IG a little. I used to be an investigator."

"Really? Cool. What made you become a chaplain?"

"It's a long, complicated story, but for most of my life I've done both."

"Both?"

"Investigation and ministry."

"Wow, very interesting. I'd like to hear that long complicated story sometime. Perhaps over dinner."

"It's a date."

She smiled. "I keep thinking about that night. Haven't really come up with anything else. It was a pretty quiet night."

"I'm still not clear on when Thomas came to the infirmary and how long he stayed."

"Thomas wasn't there on my shift," she said. "Just Johnson and Jacobson."

"What about Nurse Anderson?" I asked.

"She was in and out. Mostly out. It's what she always does—waddles around, flirts with inmates, takes smoke breaks. Anything to avoid work."

"Is there a typewriter down here?"

"I think there's an old one somewhere. We all use the computer."

"Does your inmate orderly use it?"

"Jones? I can't imagine. I don't think he reads or writes, but . . . I guess he could. I'm just not sure."

"Do you know where it is?" I asked.

"Last time I saw it . . . Think it was in the first office on the left when you enter the medical department. Just before the nurses' station. You want me to get it for you?"

"Is it locked?"

She shook her head. "Stays open. Just some extra furniture and a few supplies in there."

"Thanks. I may take a look at it. No need to take up any more of your time. But there is something you can do for me."

"Name it."

"Be extra careful," I said. "Don't be alone with anyone. This is a dangerous place."

"Prison?"

"The infirmary."

"Oh."

"Even with your orderly—"

"Jones? He's old and harmless," she said.

"Surely you don't mean—"

"I mean everyone."

"Including you?" she asked with a smile.

"I'm alone with you right now."

Now is the time for all good men to come to the aid of their country. What does it profit a man if he gains the whole world yet loses his soul? The little brown fox jumped over something or other.

After typing several sentences on the typewriter I found in the empty medical office, I pulled out one of the letters I had received and compared them.

The type was identical—the *t*'s missing the right side of the crossbar. The *o*'s missing a small place in the bottom center. And the *a*'s were darker than all the other print.

I had no way of knowing exactly who had been typing the threatening notes and sending them to me, but I now knew they had been typed here on this machine. Though it could be virtually anybody, it was most likely an inmate. A staff member could use a computer or another machine—even one outside the prison, but an inmate like Allen Jones wouldn't have access to any other machine.

40

"That's him," Kenny St. Johns said.

"You sure?" I asked.

"Yep," Lina Wilder said. "Positive. It's him."

Him was a tall, slim man with gray stubble on his gaunt face and longish, oily, unkempt gray hair.

We were sitting in Kimmy's personal car across the street from the only liquor store in town. Her patrol car would have been too suspicious.

Since the guy creeping Candace had been banned from the bar, he made daily stops by the liquor store. We had been sitting here for nearly two hours today waiting for him to come by so they could point him out to us—after waiting for over four yesterday without him showing.

The lanky man loped across the front of the store carrying a brown paper bag of booze toward his van.

"I've been thinkin'," Kenny said. "What if we tell him he's no longer banned from the bar. If he doesn't come back, then he was probably just there for Candace."

Lina said, "He could come back to look for his next victim because he took Candace and . . . killed her."

"Oh . . ." Kenny said. "Guess I didn't think it all the way through."

"It's not a bad idea," Kimmy said. "Depending on how it goes tonight . . . we might try it."

"And he never gave his name?" I asked. "Never used a credit card or—"

"Always just introduced himself as Slim. And always paid cash."

"That's not suspicious at all," Kimmy said.

"Okay," I said. "Thank you guys. We hope to have good news for you soon."

"That's it?" Lina asked.

"We don't get to do a ride along and play cops and robbers too?" Kenny said.

I didn't respond at first because I thought they were kidding, but when neither of them made a move to get out of the car, I said, "Sorry. We can't take you along. We will let you know what we find out though."

"We promise we will," Kimmy said.

"But—" Lina began.

"If you don't get out and let us get going we're going to lose him."

They began to slowly and reluctantly open their doors and climb out as Kimmy called dispatch to run Slim's plates.

"Get our girl back," Lina said.

"Let us know as soon as you know something," Kenny said. "Doesn't matter how late it is. Please."

Kimmy put the car in gear and started easing forward.

"Geez," Kenny said. "We can take a hint."

They closed the doors and we pulled out onto Main Street at a discrete distance from Slim's van.

"What's the plan, Stan?" Kimmy asked.

"Find out who he is and where he lives

for starters," I said. "So don't lose him but don't let him spot you."

Before she could respond with the sarcastic response I could see in her eyes she had at the ready, her radio sounded and dispatch reported back to her.

The van was registered to a Velvet Halliday.

"I wouldn't've figured him for a Velvet," I said.

"Velveteen maybe," Kimmy said.

"The question is . . ." I said, "is Velvet a wife or girlfriend or a victim?"

"Let's see if we can't find out," she said, and sped up a little.

To our surprise, Velvet led us to the next town over and to a busy discount grocery store there.

"Maybe he lives here," Kimmy said. "Maybe that's why nobody recognizes him over our way."

"Could be," I said. "His MO could be to live in one town and stalk women in others."

"If that's the case, he may have gotten away with it for a very long time."

"If that's what he's doing," I said, "it's possible that the van or the plates are just stolen and don't actually belong to a victim. It may be one of the ways he tries to avoid detection."

"If he is behind what happened to Candace and especially if he's done it before, he'd be right to be paranoid and cautious."

I nodded and we fell silent and stayed that way for a long while.

Eventually she said, "Oh, you know how Steve said he was asleep the night Candace went missing? And how we said one of the reasons not to suspect him was he didn't have a vehicle to get to where she was?"

"Yeah?"

"Well, I spoke to one of his neighbors again and I found out something very interesting about ol' Steve. He wasn't sleeping or vehicle-less that night. His neighbor let him borrow his old beater truck. Says he was gone for a few hours—more than enough time to go and intercept Candace and . . . do whatever was done to her."

I nodded and thought about it.

"Damn, how many people is he shopping for?"

"So *stupid*," I said.

"What?"

"I should've followed him inside. That was stupid and careless and lazy on my part. If he's a fraction as paranoid as we think he might be, I bet you anything he just ditched the van here. He's not inside shopping. He's long gone while we've been sitting here like suckers waiting on him."

While Kimmy kept watch on the van, I searched the store—carefully and thoroughly and more than once—and confirmed what I had suspected. I had let our prime suspect get away. We were no closer to finding him now than we had been days ago. All I had done was wasted time we didn't have and blew our best chance of catching him.

Over the next few days we continued to stake out the liquor store—sitting on it for even longer periods of time thanks to deputies in plain clothes using impounded vehicles—but he never showed again.

We continued to search for him and to issue BOLOs around the state, but nothing we did yielded any results.

He had vanished just like Candace had, and he was just as gone as she was.

41

Confinement felt even more dark and oppressive today.

When I signed in at the sergeant's desk, I told him I had received a note from the first shift sergeant asking me to check on an inmate named Larkins.

He nodded and gave me the cell number.

I thanked him and headed toward Larkins's cell.

About halfway down the long hallway, a small group of inmates appeared, stepping out of dark cells into the dim corridor.

The confinement cells were supposed to remain locked at all times. No inmates should be out of their cells, in a group, in the hall.

I glanced back at the sergeant's desk. He was gone.

When I looked back at the group of inmates they were moving toward me, closing in, having picked up their pace.

Continuing to face them, I began to move back toward the empty desk—not that being down there would be any better than here. I was locked in with no way of escape.

Behind the group of inmates I caught sight of an officer.

At first I felt relief but it was quickly replaced by a sinking dread as I saw that it was Captain Matthew Skipper.

In another few moments, the inmates had me surrounded.

Skipper stepped into the circle with me.

"Chaplain, I hear you're confused about exactly what your job is around here," he said, his breath smelling of tobacco and coffee.

He was probably six-four, but he slumped, as if the weight of his belly was pulling him forward.

"Thought I'd remind you," he said.

"You're here to give this bunch of degenerates some religion. That's it. Nothing else."

I didn't say anything.

"I think you're in serious need of some job counseling."

"That what these men do?" I asked, nodding toward the inmates circling us. "Career counseling."

"When it's needed."

"You should speak to the warden about my job description."

"Stone? He's a prissy little pussy. Thinks he's HNIC around here, but everybody knows I run this bitch."

"And doing a mighty fine job of it," I said.

"You got a complaint or a suggestion, now's the time. These boys are also my complaints department."

Before I could respond, he stepped aside and the circle closed in on me.

The first blow was a body shot that caught me in the kidney. It was a hard blow, well delivered, and I wondered if the guy who threw it had been trained as a boxer.

My knees buckled and I started down.

One of them caught me, lifted me back

up, and then punched me hard under the chin.

Head ringing. Room spinning.

I held up my hands in an attempt to block some of the blows, but it did little good.

The next time my legs gave, no one caught me.

I hit the bare, rough concrete floor hard and they started kicking me.

My vision was blurred as I covered my head with my arms and pulled my legs up into a fetal position for protection.

"Inmates," I heard someone yell. "Inmates, face the wall with your hands behind your head. NOW. Captain, I'll have you and the chaplain secure in just a moment," the officer said.

I looked up. Skipper punched one of the inmates in the face and began to yell. "Get against the fucking wall, motherfuckers. Do it. Now. Or I kill every last one of you sons of bitches."

I WAS in Medical being treated by Sandy

Strickland, Anna next to her watching her work.

I felt like I had just been fifteen rounds with Foreman. In actuality, I only had a cut under my chin and a small abrasion on my right cheek. I had no idea where the captain was, but I found myself periodically looking over my shoulder.

"Funny how the captain didn't sustain any injuries at all, isn't it?" Anna said.

"Funny ha ha or not funny at all?" I said.

"You must be feeling okay if you can make jokes," Anna said.

"I feel okay. How do I look?"

"Still the best-looking man in the institution," Anna said.

"Best looking maybe, most beat-up certainly," Sandy said.

42

When I arrived at the warden's office, he was seated behind his desk, Tom Daniels and Pete Fortner, the institutional inspector, in front of it.

"Have a—" Stone began. "What happened to you? You been fighting?"

I sat down between Daniels and Fortner and told them I was attacked in Confinement.

"Pattern of behavior," Daniels said.

Stone nodded.

"What's that?"

Stone looked at Daniels.

Daniels said, "Chaplain Jordan, we've received some very serious allegations concerning your conduct while an employee of the Department of Corrections. We've made the decision to suspend you without pay until a thorough investigation can be conducted."

"What?" I asked, finding it difficult to speak or even swallow. "Are you serious?"

"We're taking this very seriously."

"Like you did the allegations against Shutt and Skipper?" I said.

"Unlike them, there's actual evidence against you, not just allegations and speculation."

"Evidence of what?"

Daniels flipped through a few papers in an open file folder on his lap.

"An inmate's wife has accused you of assault and rape in the chapel and having her husband locked up and threatened in order to keep her quiet."

"I told you who she said did that. I had you process the crime scene."

"A very smart and calculating move," Daniels said. "I'd expect no less from you."

"Chaplain, look at it from our perspective," Stone said. "She's putting a lot of pressure on Tallahassee. Demanding her husband be released from lockup and a full investigation be conducted. She's gone to the press. The department has to act quickly and decisively. We'll get to the bottom of it and if you're innocent—"

"*If*," I said. "*If*. This is . . ."

"Listen to me, Chaplain," Stone said. "Don't make this any worse than it is. Lie low. Let us investigate. I promise you the truth will come out."

Fortner finally spoke up. "I know you think this is personal because of your history with Inspector Daniels, but I'd have to handle things the same way based on the victim's testimony and the evidence we have."

"You said you found semen and blood," I said. "Test it. She told me her husband raped her. I'm sure you'll find it's his."

"You willing to provide a sample too?" Daniels said.

"Absolutely. But to FDLE, not you."

43

The thing I wanted to do most—confront Molly Thomas—I couldn't do.

It would only make things worse.

So would having Dad or someone in his department talk to her.

I was driving my old S-10 in the direction of town, but it was only a direction, not a destination. I had nowhere to go, nowhere to be.

I considered calling Susan to ask her to talk to her dad. What had she told him about what happened between us to get him to do what he's doing? I hadn't spoken to her in over a year and had no desire to do so now, but I was desperate.

In town I pulled into the Jr. Mart parking lot and used the pay phone to call her.

She didn't answer.

I got back in my truck and considered driving up to the state park, but instead I just drove.

Eventually I wound up at Potter's Landing, some ten miles outside town.

I started to make a U-turn, to head back into town, waiting long enough for a white Ford Bronco to pass by.

But it didn't.

It slowed and pulled off the road at an angle blocking me in.

Matt Skipper and three other men, including Shutt, got out.

I tried to think whether there was anything in my truck I could use for a weapon. The tire iron was the only thing that came to mind, but it was latched inside a recessed storage spot in the back. I could never get it out in time.

I jammed the gear shifter in Reverse and stomped on the gas.

But before I had moved very far, Skipper

was there pointing a handgun at my head through the open window.

"Stop and put it in Park," he said.

Without waiting for me to, he reached in, grabbed me, and starting pulling me out.

With my truck still rolling backward, Shutt rushed over and helped him pull me the rest of the way out through the window.

Once I was clear of the truck, they slung me toward the road. I hit the pavement hard and rolled a few times, scraping my hands and arms and face as I did.

Using my momentum, I pushed myself up and started to run.

That's when one of the other men stepped up and clocked me on the nose with a tire iron he swung like a baseball bat.

Blood spurted out. Cartilage crunched. My eyes filled with tears. Shooting pain. Disorientation. Nausea. Dizziness. Blurred vision.

As I pitched forward, he swung again, striking me just as hard as before, this time in the abdomen.

I went down hard, unable to breathe, throwing up as I did.

I knelt there vomiting for a moment and trying to catch my breath.

"Twenty bucks to whoever can guess what he had for lunch," Skipper said.

On my last heave, I pitched forward.

With everything in me, I tried to get up, but I couldn't.

"Search the truck," Skipper said.

As they did, I lay there with tears, blood, and vomit smeared on my face, unable to move, unable to take a deep breath.

"It's not here, boss," Shutt said.

"Get him up," Skipper yelled.

He got right in front of me after two of his men were holding me vertically again. "Where're the tapes, you son of a bitch?"

I thought I responded, but evidently nothing came out.

"Answer me," he said.

I tried to again.

He stepped aside and the two men holding me went to work.

One got behind me to hold my hands back as the other one moved into position in front of me.

The guy in front used my midsection like

a heavy-bag while the officer behind me held me up.

I began to heave again. This time only blood came out.

"My turn," the guy behind me said.

He let me go and I crumpled to the ground.

They switched positions, then yanked me up again.

The guy in front said, "Hold him still. I held him still for you."

The officer holding me began to move me from side to side as if I were a boxer bobbing and weaving.

"Cut it out," the one in front said.

They guy holding me didn't.

This frustrated the guy in front, and he took it out on me.

After missing me a few times, he finally connected with a hard, perfectly placed shot to my chin, and I lost consciousness.

44

I awoke to the muddy, muted sounds of soft, constant beeps, whispering voices, and the low hum of an air conditioner.

Everything sounded as if it was under water.

When my eyes finally opened, they closed again from the assault of the bright light.

"Close the blinds. He's waking up."

I opened my eyes again, blinking against the light, less bright now.

A TV mounted on the wall in front of me was tuned to CNN.

I lifted my right hand. Something was

attached to my forefinger. I tried to remove it, but a hand descended and prevented me.

My eyes followed the hand up the arm to the body to which it was attached. It was a beautiful goddess with large brown eyes and long brown hair. Beside her was another one.

Anna and Laura.

A voice from the other side of the bed said something I didn't catch. I turned toward it to see Merrill standing there with a wide grin on his face.

"How do you feel?" one of the ladies asked.

I turned in that direction again, which didn't take any more than five minutes.

"Like I just went fifteen rounds with Foreman," I said.

"Look it, too," Merrill said. "If big George was fighting with a tire iron."

"Anna, Merrill, this is Laura Matthers. Laura, this is Anna and Merrill."

They all laughed. "We know each other pretty well by now," Anna said.

"We've been in here all up in each other's business for three days," Merrill said.

"I don't remember."

"You've been resting," Laura said.

I was puzzled, which must have registered on my face.

"You been out cold, man," Merrill said.

"What? For three days?"

They all nodded.

Something was on my nose. I reached up to touch it. Some sort of plastic device was taped to it.

I could tell that both of my eyes were black and that various bandages covered various abrasions on my face. The underside of my chin was split open pretty bad, but there didn't seem to be any stitches, just butterfly Band-Aids.

"Why didn't they kill me?"

"Some badass Negro in a big-ass pimp-mobile-looking car scared 'em off."

"What were you doing driving Uncle Tyrone's car?" I asked.

"He needed my truck to haul his old lady's dresser. She leavin' again. Twice every year he has to borrow that shit to move her shit, then borrow it again to move her ass back in. Anna told me what happened. I went out lookin' for you. I made a lot of noise coming in—horn honking, firing a gun. They took off."

"White flight," I said.

He smiled.

"You see who it was?"

"Affirmative. They sittin' up in your daddy's jail right now—well, all but Skipper. He came up with an ironclad alibi and none of his helpers gonna roll over on him—even though they may be some police brutality goin' on up in there."

"Mom," I whispered when I had rolled up beside her bed.

It was late the next night. I was in a wheelchair in my mom's room on the next floor down.

She didn't respond.

She was on her side, her back to me. She was emaciated. Her hospital gown, which she should not have had to wear because I should have brought her one from home, was tied only at the top.

"Mom," I said a little louder this time.

She slowly raised her head and then let it fall back down again. I wheeled around to the other side of the bed.

"Mom," I said even louder, and this time directly toward her wrinkled, seemingly life-less face.

Her eyes opened, and in them I saw misery and confusion and fear.

She closed her eyes.

The closeness of our eyes seemed to make her uncomfortable.

She probably needed a drink. I know I did.

I rolled the chair back slightly. This time when she opened her eyes, that's how they stayed.

"John," she said, her voice warm and re-freshingly sober. "What happened to you? What's wrong?"

"Sorry it took me so long to get here," I said.

"It's okay, honey."

"Sorry for how I spoke to you on the phone the other night."

"I'm sorry for all I've put you through. You've always been such a kind, sensitive young man. Had to be . . . so hard. I see now how . . . Can you . . . Will you forgive me?"

And though it wasn't the end of the pain or resentment, it was the beginning of the end.

45

I was lying on my couch, propped up on several pillows on Saturday afternoon, reading a stack of newspapers.

My entire body was stiff and sore, every movement bringing about pain and discomfort.

All the area papers reported about the same things—I had been suspended pending an investigation into sexual assault allegations. A few added that though I had never been charged, similar allegations of sexual misconduct had occurred when I was pastoring in Atlanta. There was no mention of the Atlanta Child Murders or the Stone Cold Killer case or anything else about my

work at the Stone Mountain Police Department.

I was nearly finished reading the mostly
fact-free articles when someone knocked on
my door.

"It's open," I yelled, not wanting to get up.
"Come in."

A young woman with light blond hair,
pale white skin, and light blue eyes came in.
She was wearing a blue business suit
roughly the color of her eyes, and I thought I
detected a shoulder holster beneath her
jacket.

"John Jordan," she said as she walked
in, "I'm Rachel Mills, an agent with the
Florida   Department   of   Law
Enforcement."

"Have a seat."

"I'm looking into the accusations that you
sexually assaulted the wife of an inmate in
the chapel of Potter Correctional Institution.
I'm just in search of the truth. Not trying to
jam you up. Far as I'm concerned, you're absolutely   innocent   until   evidence   says
otherwise."

"Then I'll remain innocent, because
there is no evidence."

She nodded. "Everybody says that. Convince me by answering some questions."

"Okay."

"Where were you the Monday night of the Ike Johnson murder? By the way, do you mind if I tape this?"

She pulled out a microcassette recorder and pressed Record.

"No, I don't mind. I was at an AA meeting in a Sunday school room at the First Methodist Church of Panama City, Florida, from six until eight. I then went to Applebee's on Twenty-third Street with two of the members. I then drove home, arriving about twelve forty-five. I read a little and then went to bed . . . alone."

"Can someone corroborate your story?" she asked.

"AA is anonymous. It would be their choice, but I'll ask."

"It's not that important. The crime occurred far later than that anyway, but if they're willing, it wouldn't hurt. Did you speak to anyone after you got home that night who could confirm your whereabouts?"

"No."

She started to say something but I stopped her.

"The thing about both the murder of Ike Johnson and the assault on Molly Thomas," I said, "is that they both took place inside the prison. I wasn't inside the prison when either happened. And anyone who was, including the killer, was logged in at the control room."

She nodded. "That's a good point. How well do you know Molly Thomas?"

"I've probably spent a sum total of three or four hours with her. Most of that time has been in the visiting park of the institution. I've counseled her and her husband during some of their visits together, at their request, of course. They, like most inmate couples, were having some marital problems and wanted my help."

"Were you able to help them?"

"Apparently not. I thought so at first, but then lately something has happened to Anthony, her husband. He's on a serious downward spiral."

"Have you ever met with Molly Thomas by herself at or away from the institution?"

I nodded. "Yes, I have. Friday before last. She called and asked to see me, saying it was an emergency and she was scared to come to the institution. So we met in the pastor's office of the Methodist church in Pottersville."

"What was the nature of that meeting?"

"She described what took place at the institution the night of her assault and how Captain Matthew Skipper followed her home and tried to force his way into her house. She asked for my help."

"Who did she say raped her?"

"Her husband."

"He's an inmate. How could he have even seen her?"

"Captain Skipper arranged it, according to her, but interrupted them in the middle and then stalked her that night and tried to break into her home."

"Why didn't you come forward with this information?"

"I did. I told the inspector general of the department, Tom Daniels, and the warden of PCI, Edward Stone."

She was about to say something else when my phone rang.

"Sorry, but with everything going on, I

need to get it," I said.

She nodded.

I answered the phone.

It was Sandy Strickland.

"How are you?" she asked.

"I've been better."

"I stopped by the hospital to see you, but . . . you were still unconscious."

"Thanks for coming by. I really appreciate that."

"I . . ."

"What is it?" I asked.

"I'm hearing and reading some pretty horrible things."

"I know. But they're not true. And I know everybody always says that but . . . they really aren't."

"One time, sure, but . . . when there's a pattern."

"There's not. Truly."

"Anyway, that's not why I called. If you are innocent . . . makes this even more difficult to do now, but . . ."

"Sandy, please listen to me. I didn't do— Makes what more difficult to do?"

"Your first test came back . . ."

My heart started banging and I found it

difficult to breathe.

"It was positive for the HIV infection."

"What?" I whispered as the breath suddenly rushed out of me.

"I know this is the worst possible time . . . which I guess only matters if you're innocent."

"I am," I said, "but that hardly matters now."

When she hung up, I sat there with the phone still at my ear, unable to move.

"You okay?" Rachel Mills asked.

"Huh? Oh. Can we do this later? I need to—"

"Just a couple more questions. Okay?"

Though I gave no indication that it was, she pressed on.

"Was there anyone present at your meeting with Molly Thomas at the church?"

"Yes. I'd never meet with the wife of an inmate alone. The pastor of the church, the Reverend Dick Clydesdale, was in the next office monitoring the session, and I told Molly that he was."

"Would you be willing to submit blood and semen samples? If you're telling the truth, it will clear this up quickly."

I nodded. "Gladly. Because *I'm* telling the truth."

"I sincerely hope so. It would be a refreshing change."

46

"We came to say goodbye," Colby said. "We go to meet our new foster family tomorrow."

Something inside me broke a little, and I couldn't speak for a moment.

Eventually I managed, "I'm so, so sorry I haven't found your mom yet, but . . . I'm not going to stop until I do. I promise you that. I won't stop looking. No matter what."

"What happened to you?" Cody asked.

"I was in a little car accident . . ."

"Is that where you've been?" Colby asked. "You just disappeared on us."

"I'm so sorry. I was in the hospital and I was in and out of consciousness. I would've called if I could have. Ms. Kimmy and Mr. Merrill said they have been checking on you."

"Are you okay?" Colby asked.

I nodded. "I am. I'm hurting far more on the inside that y'all are leaving."

"Thank you for all you've done for us," she said. "For all you've done to try to find her."

I couldn't tell if Colby was angry at me or attempting stoicism.

"I mean it," I said. "I won't stop."

"We know."

"I'll be checking on y'all too," I said. "Making sure you're okay. I'll even work it out so I can pick you guys up and take you out."

"For pizza?" she said.

And tears filled our eyes at the same time.

"Are you sure we can't just stay here with you?" Cody said.

"*Cody*," Colby said. "I told you not to . . . that we weren't going to ask him again."

"If there was any way," I said. "Any way at all . . . There's nothing I'd like better than to have you guys here all the time."

"Just 'til you find our mom," Cody said. "That won't be long, will it?"

"I . . . I hope it won't be," I said.

"Well, we've got to go," Colby said.

"So soon?"

"We haven't finished packing yet."

"Y'all do know it's not up to me, right?" I said. "If it were, y'all would already be living here."

"Couldn't you . . ." Colby began. "I mean . . . What if *you* become a foster parent?"

"Yeah," Cody said. "You be our foster dad."

"I would in a heartbeat if they'd let me," I said. "They won't let single men be—"

"Couldn't you marry someone?" Cody said. "Just 'til our mom gets back. *Oooh*, then you could marry her."

Colby took her brother by the hand. "I'll explain it to him," she said, and began to lead him away.

Tears streaming down my cheeks, I walked them to the door and gave them both hugs. "I'll see you real soon," I said. "Hopefully with your mom."

47

Unable to sleep, unable to stop thinking about Colby and Cody being in a strange new environment and how they must feel utterly and completely alone, rejected, abandoned, motherless, and hopeless, I drove back out to the old collapsing barn on 73 to look around again.

Unlike when I was out here previously, the moon was bigger and stars filled the night sky. There was more light on the scene. I could see more. But there wasn't more to see.

Why was the car backed into the barn? Why were the headlights and blinker on? Surely her abductor or killer would want the car concealed as long as possible. *Why was the car moved and put back again? How was she abducted so quickly? Where was she headed that night? Who was she going to see? Was she really leaving, headed over to Hope House without Colby and Cody?*

And while I'm asking questions— Why must the innocent suffer? Why do our children pay the penalty for our wickedness? Why do Colby and Cody have to be without their mother right now? Why do they have to be without a dad all the time? What is wrong with this world that things could be this way for them?

What if nothing was what it seemed? Start there. What if nothing with her car was what it looked like? What would that change? What if Candace wasn't what she looked like?

Maybe everything and everyone was just what it looked like. But if it wasn't, what does it change? It would be easier to figure out what was going on and where Candace was if everything or nothing was what it seemed, but what if only certain things were or weren't what they seemed? Where does that leave me?

Would Candace really leave without her children? Why? What was so unbearable that she would try to escape this life? And did she? Or did something or someone happen to prevent her from making her getaway? And if so, who?

As usual I had far more questions than answers, but plaguing me even more than my many questions were my worries for Colby and Cody and the way my heart was breaking for them, and the way I was powerless to do anything for them—except finding their mother, something I was failing miserably at.

48

On Sunday afternoon, in record-setting heat, I was lying under a tall bald cypress tree near the bank of the Apalachicola River, my head on Laura's lap.

Laura's lap wasn't as comfortable or as soft as the stack of pillows back on my couch. There were, however, other consolations.

The base of the bald cypress swelled to four times the circumference of the rest of the trunk, and there were cypress knees shooting up all around it. The grayish-brown, spiraling base of the tree was normally covered in water, but the summer was dry, the river low.

A small breeze rippled the surface of the coffee-colored water and waved the Spanish moss hanging from the craggy cypress branches above us.

"I moved to Atlanta right after high school," I said. "The night I graduated, in fact. I was obsessed with the Atlanta Child Murders. Had an encounter with Wayne Williams as a kid. I've always done some form of both investigation and ministry— even back then. Went to seminary school while working a couple of cases. Eventually became a cop in Stone Mountain and later a pastor. I was drinking on and off. A few of the investigations I worked were particularly horrific and difficult. When I transitioned to mostly ministry, I stopped drinking, threw myself into my work, and ignored how ill-suited my wife and I were."

"You exchanged one addiction for another," she said.

I nodded. "I was a classic workaholic, seduced by the incredible feeling helping people can give. This whole time I'd been living as a dry drunk, and that was okay with Susan, my ex-wife, because that's what she was used to. We had a nice, comfortable, unhealthy relationship. We didn't see each other all that much, and we lived in a glass house, so when we did, we were usually doing our best to look our best. Finally, everything started stacking up—the pressure of being a pastor, of trying to meet all the needs of a large congregation, unable to say no—and this after never really having processed the bad cases. I started drinking again —which is just a symptom of . . . other deeper issues. Susan was a classic, well-trained enabler. She was the best. The silence, the secrets, the excuses, and the justification. But eventually I started AA again— read the books, got a sponsor, and became honest about my addiction. Something both Susan and my congregation couldn't tolerate."

Upstream, a fish jumped and made a loud splash.

"When I was accused of having an affair with one of my parishioners, Susan was so insecure, so . . . disconnected from me . . . she believed it and made everything worse."

"Why did the woman accuse you of adultery?"

"She didn't. Her husband did. She had

come to see me because they were both severe addicts. She wanted help. He didn't. So
he . . . Not too long after that, she committed
suicide. He said she had done it because I
had . . . Anyway, the papers smeared me with
rumors and innuendo and . . . I . . . just didn't
have it in me to fight any of them anymore."

"Them?"

"The members of my congregation who
wanted me gone. The church hierarchy. The
media. Susan. I resigned the church. We divorced. I came home."

THE WALK back to my trailer was short but
slow.

Every step hurt, but was worth it for all
the good the sun and river and Laura's lap
had done for me.

When we neared the trailer I could hear
the phone ringing.

Though it took us a while to get there, it
was still ringing when we did.

Long before I picked up the receiver, I
knew it was going to be bad news—so I
wasn't shocked or even surprised, only sad-
dened, when it came.

It was Merrill. He was violating a direct order by calling to tell me that Anthony Thomas had been murdered in the infirmary the night before—stabbed and raped with a surgical scalpel, which the murderer had left in the body.

49

"You look awful," Molly Thomas said.

She was seated in the only chair in my living room, wearing a pair of dark blue jeans, a white oxford button-down shirt, and white leather Keds.

When she'd knocked on the door, Laura had let her in, not realizing who she was. Apart from her clothes, she looked like the grieving widow she was. Her eyes were deep and hollow with large dark circles beneath them. Her auburn hair was thin and wispy, part of it standing up, and she had aged ten years in the ten days since I had last seen her.

"I don't think it's a good idea for you to

be here," I said. "I'm very sorry about Anthony, but I'm not the one to help you right now."

"I've got to talk to you," she said, her voice flat, her face expressionless. "I know what I've put you through, but I'm going to make it right. I wanted you to know I was sorry. I just didn't know what else to do."

Laura stood near the door, watching, listening, protecting.

"I was just trying to protect Tony, to get him transferred to another institution. Away from Skipper."

I nodded.

"It didn't work. Obviously. It got him killed. But I'm gonna make it right. I mean for you."

"I doubt what you did got Anthony killed. The things he's been doing, the men he's involved with . . ."

"He wasn't this bad when he went to prison. I mean, he was . . . He had his issues, but . . . the last time I saw him . . . That was someone else entirely."

"I'm sorry."

"I'm gonna make it right," she said. "Tell the authorities and the press. I've wronged

you more than any other person ever. I just . .
. It was all to try to save Tony."

LATER IN THE AFTERNOON, while Laura was
helping her mother go through her Uncle
Russ's things, Anna came over to watch the
tapes from Russ Maddox's house that Dad
had dropped by earlier.

"You sure you want to do this?" I asked.

She nodded. "Don't move. I've got this."

She placed the tapes in a stack on top of
the television—an old thirteen-inch TV on
an old-fashioned TV stand with a VCR on
the uneven shelf below it.

"Dad said he appreciated us doing this.
Said he was having a hard time getting
anyone in his department to watch them."

The first tape was the one I had already
seen. It showed Maddox and Johnson together again. We didn't watch very much of it
—I had seen it, and Anna wanted to see as
little as possible. I couldn't blame her. We
watched roughly two minutes of it. They
were the last two minutes though, and when
she ejected the tape, I noticed that there was
at least three quarters of the tape unused.

I eased off the couch and put the tape back in and began to fast forward it. The snow on the screen looked no different in the fast forward mode than it did in the normal play mode, with the exception of the lines at the top and bottom of the screen that looked like wrinkles.

After about five minutes or so, I ejected the tape, concluding that there was nothing else on it.

The second tape was of Maddox alone.

When the first image flickered on the screen, it was of Maddox's bare chest. It was roughly the color of cotton and covered with white hair. He was obviously leaning over the camera to turn it on. He then backed up, bent down, and looked right into the lens, his fat, out-of-focus face filling the screen. I could see the reflection of the red recording light flashing on his left cheek. He turned and headed toward the bed, and the light could then be seen flashing on his other left cheek.

Waiting on the bed for him were a re-mote control and a jar of Vaseline. He pointed the remote in the direction of the camera, and the TV began to play. The sounds of sex began to fill the speakers. They sounded as if they were coming from his TV, and because the video camera was so close to the TV the sound was distorted, but it was still unmistakable. It sounded like the tape we had just watched. Russ was watching himself with Johnson.

He removed the lid from the Vaseline jar, scooped out a heaping amount, and began to masturbate.

I fast-forwarded through the rest, only glancing occasionally to make sure there wasn't anything of evidentiary value on the tape.

"It's so personal," Anna said. "Even more so than watching two people have sex. It's personal and private and in this case kinda sad."

I nodded. "Yes it is."

The third tape was Maddox and Johnson again. It was shot in black and white, which, because of the contrast between the two men, looked almost artistic.

The last tape showed Maddox with Anthony Thomas.

Thomas wasn't the willing participant Johnson seemed to be, and though it was obvious he was in a drug-altered state, there was still a lot of coercion and even a little force.

When we finished watching the tapes, I felt like I needed a shower.

"Whatta you think?" Anna asked.

"I think what you think. Everybody on these tapes is now dead."

"Skipper is running a sex slave ring," she said. "It's an utterly evil abuse of power and—"

"Weren't there five tapes?" I said.

"I left one of the cases in the box," she said. "Had a smaller tape inside. Figured it was an audio tape or—"

"Can I see?"

She retrieved the tape and brought it over to me. It was not an audiotape, but an eight-millimeter videotape.

"It's eight millimeter," I said.

"What does that mean?"

"It's video but from a different camera than the one in Maddox's bedroom. It's not standard VHS like these other tapes. It means that it was shot by somebody else."

"Let's watch it."

I laughed. "It takes a different type of VCR."

"Who would have one?"

"Susan still has ours."

"Wanna ride up to Atlanta and see if she'll loan it to us?"

Just then the phone rang, and I knew it was bad news again. I was almost to the point of not answering my phone anymore.

It was Dad.

Molly Thomas was dead.

50

Under the massive spreading branches of a live oak tree near the bald cypresses lining the banks, Molly Thomas's car was being pulled out of the muddy waters of the Apalachicola River.

The crooked, craggy cypresses, both in and out of the water, were silhouettes against the neon orange and pink of the setting sun.

The swirling, undulating waters patted the red clay of the banks in this picturesque spot, where I had learned to water-ski and later had been baptized.

It appears that Molly's car had raced down the hill at high speed and crashed into the river below.

The yellow crime-scene tape, stretched between two cypress trees near the water, rippled in the small breeze coming off the water, making a small, lonely whipping sound.

Molly's car could just be seen breaking the surface of the water. A cable attached to her back bumper was spinning around the winch of the tow truck, pulling the two vehicles ever closer to one another.

At certain points along the way, the steady hum of the winch was interrupted by the grinding of metal on metal as the river begrudgingly released the car.

"This the girl you were dickin'?" Jake asked when I walked up to where he, Dad, and two other officers stood.

Jake and the two officers laughed.

"Does it look like suicide?" I asked Dad, ignoring Jake.

He nodded. "No signs she tried to brake or that another vehicle was involved."

"You were such a bad lay that she offed herself," Jake said to even more laughter.

"Okay to walk down there?" I asked Dad.

He nodded. "Sure."

I slowly walked down to the river's edge,

feeling awkward and self-conscious, stiff and sore.

The car was out of the water now.

Molly's wet auburn hair was matted and hung forward with the rest of her slumping body only held vertical by the seatbelt. The hair covered her face. For that I was glad.

The driver's side door was open, the ME beginning to examine the body. Water was still draining onto the ground.

The strong odor of the river emanated from the car, the smell of fish and tannin and mildew.

I walked around to the back of the car and studied the bumper.

It was bent slightly, but there was no way to know when it had happened.

There were a few dents and some white paint from another vehicle on the back right quarter panel. The paint could have been on the car for six months or six hours. There was no way to know for sure. But I knew.

This was the work of Matt Skipper.

51

The Quarters, the name given to the black section of town by a certain segment of the white population, was roughly two hundred acres on the south side of Pottersville, only part of which was inside the city limits. A single row of small red-brick duplexes provided by the government for low-income housing was the only part of black Pottersville actually located within Pottersville.

The low-income housing, known as the black projects, was a mirror image of the government housing on the east side of town, known as the white projects. The only difference in the two projects was color. It was more like a negative than a mirror—the negative of a hateful and ugly picture of racism, tribalism, and xenophobia.

I drove past the row of identical duplexes and found myself again surprised by how widely the yards varied. In front of most of the dwellings, the yards were barren, a mixture of dirt, weeds, and trash. Others, however, had neatly trimmed lawns and a shrub or two. Most of the houses did not have vehicles in front of them. Of those that did, many were tireless heaps up on blocks and covered with plastic tarps. Two of the units had late-model Cadillacs that gleamed even under the late-evening sun.

On the corner, around a small fire, three men and a woman—all holding tall beer cans or bottles in paper bags in their hands.

Across the road and down two yards, at least twenty children were playing various games under the watchful eye of an elderly gray-haired lady rocking on her front porch and occasionally leaning forward and spitting snuff into the front yard.

When I arrived at Uncle Tyrone's house, his numerous children sitting on his front porch told me that Merrill and Tyrone were already at his shop.

Before I joined them in the shop, I stepped inside the house and used the phone.

Kimmy answered after one ring.

"Had a thought," I said.

"Let's hear it."

"It was something the highway patrol officer said. My subconscious must have connected it while I was in the hospital. He said he stopped at the scene when he saw me because he thought I might be the killer returning to the scene."

"Yeah?" she said. "They do that sometimes."

"What if our witness wasn't a witness, but the killer?" I said.

"Who?"

"Lance Stephenson," I said. "He took pictures and everything."

"Certainly possible," she said. "Worth looking at him again."

"Who interviewed him?" I asked.

"Cecil," she said.

"Who is a teetotaler and has probably

never stepped foot in the Sports Oasis," I said.

"Yeah?"

"What if Creepy Carl or Velvet, as you and I were calling him, is Lance Stephenson?"

"Oh shit," she said.

"Since he gave an official statement," I said, "there's a chance that Lance Stephenson is his real name or at least that he gave a real phone number. Y'all should be able to track him by either."

"I'm on it," she said. "I'm all over it. I'll let you know what I find out."

Stepping back out onto the porch, I thanked the kids for the use of the phone and headed back to the workshop.

Uncle Tyrone owned a shoe shop just over the tracks in Pottersville. This meant that although he lived on the wrong side of the tracks, Tyrone owned his own business on the right side of the tracks. His was one of only four black-owned businesses in Pottersville and the only one that was located in the white part of Pottersville.

He wasn't very far across the tracks, but it was far enough to suit him and close enough to the tracks to suit the white establishment. I had heard some of that white establishment refer to him as a "white negra." No one had ever said anything like that to me, because they knew what I was—what I had been labeled since the eighth grade when I had fallen in love with Merrill's little sister, Kyria—a nigger lover.

"Cousin John," Tyrone said as I walked in, giving me his usual greeting. "How ya be, boy? Not lookin' too good there."

"I'm okay, Uncle Tyrone. How are you?"

"I'm hangin' tough. Hangin' tough. So let me see your tape. Is it standard eight millimeter or high eight?"

I reached into my pocket and retrieved the tape. "Standard," I said as I handed him the tape.

"Ah, yeah, I can handle this. Right back here."

He walked through the faded curtain behind the counter. Merrill and I followed.

In the back of Tyrone's store was an office roughly the size of my trailer. It was filled with shelves, which were filled with shoe boxes. On a table that stood against the right wall, there were all sorts of electronic equipment—VCRs, TVs, and stereo components. The eight-millimeter VCR sat on top of a small, square monitor in the center of the table.

"You the only white man who come in here," he said, smiling broadly. "Any other think I stole all this shit for sure." We all laughed, though it was more true than funny.

He popped the tape in.

"I have no idea what's on the tape. Would you mind if Merrill and I previewed it alone?"

"Just push Play when you're ready," he said, and left the room.

I did.

The first scene to fill the screen was of a floor whose carpet looked familiar to me. It was the chapel at PCI. There was very little light, the picture on the screen dark and grainy. When the camera tilted up and panned left, it showed Molly Thomas walking hesitantly into the dark chapel. She was shivering.

Within seconds, Anthony had pounced on her and began to rape her. She didn't scream very loudly, but you could tell that she was in pain. In between the screams, she tried to reason with Anthony.

They seemed unaware of the camera's presence in the sanctuary. One time Anthony looked straight at it without looking into it. His eyes were wild, darting back and forth, glazed and icy as frozen ponds. In a few moments, Skipper came in and snatched them both up, laughing and taunting them as he did.

The small video did two things. It showed that I was not involved, and that Skipper was. Unfortunately, Skipper was only shown as breaking up the violation and not as instigating it.

Within another minute, the chapel was empty, and the camera stopped recording. The monitor went blue. I let the tape play a little longer then stopped it. The whole incident lasted less than five minutes.

"Looks like your ass just been cleared," Merrill said. "Got that Rodney King shit."

52

"When I worked for the Stone Mountain Police Department," I said, "I obeyed the law and mostly all the rules. I knew what I could do and what I couldn't. What would jeopardize a case. What would jeopardize my job."

Before we left Uncle Tyrone's, I had asked Merrill to drop by when he could. At the time I had asked him to because I wanted to run a new theory I had about Candace's case by him, but by the time he had arrived I had convinced myself it was right and all that was left to do was act on it—test it, so to speak.

We were standing in my small kitchen having a glass of iced tea.

"Criminals got a big advantage over cops," he said.

I nodded. "I'm not a cop right now," I said.

"No, you're not."

"Just a regular ol' citizen."

He smiled. "John Q. Public."

"I can do things as a citizen I couldn't do as a cop," I said.

"And you should."

"I know—or think I do—what happened to Candace," I said. "It's not enough for a warrant."

"But John Q. don't need one."

"It's probably not even enough to justify an interview by the police," I said. "And if it was, I'm afraid of what that might make him do. So, I'm going in—going to actually break in to test my theory. Because that's all it is. I'm gonna see if I'm right. If I'm not, hopefully I can get out without anyone ever knowing."

"'Cept me," he said.

"'Cept you," I said. "I was counting on you not running to the police to turn me in."

"You underestimating how seriously I take my job as a confidential informant."

I laughed. "Thing is . . . I'd feel better about having someone to back my play," I said. "Wouldn't have to break in with me or even break any laws, just wait outside, keep watch, help out if things go south."

"And?"

"And I was wondering what you were doing tonight," I said.

"I'a tell you what my black ass is not doin'," he said. "Not gonna be some playin' it safe lookout backup bitch, I can tell you that. I goin' . . . I goin' in—full partner in this criminal enterprise. So quit wastin' time with all this talk-talk and let's ride. You can tell me who you think it is and why on the way."

53

"I thought it might be the witness Lance Stephenson," I said. "Thought he might be the customer who had creeped out Candace, but now who I *think* it is—or who I think I know it is—*is* Kenny St. John."

Merrill and I were racing to the old house Kenny shared with his elderly mom out by Alabama Landing.

"*Why* is for many, many reasons," I continued, "some I can't even adequately explain. But the woman at Hope House, Wendy, said that Candace told her a friend was going to help her make her escape. Who better than a gay best friend? I think Kenny very subtly pretends to be gay as a way of hiding his sick proclivities. I think he was the friend helping her escape, and the secret nature of it inspired him to act and aided him in what he did. I think he gave Lina a ride home, which was part of his alibi, and then went to meet Candace—which is how they planned it in order to keep her disappearance mysterious and a secret—even from Lina. Candace thought he was meeting her to help her stage her abandoned car and then drive her to Hope House. But after they staged the car and she got in his with him, something the search dogs showed us she did, everything changed for her and all she did was wake from a bad dream to enter a new nightmare. I'm hoping that what he did was abduct her, imprison her, and not kill her. When his mom woke to answer Lina's call, I bet he was just getting back home. When he and Lina and Kimmy went out looking for Candace, he already had her— either in his trunk, in a hole somewhere, or chained up at his home. I'm really hoping we find her alive in his home. That's why I want to go in now and not wait. If she is alive I don't want to risk him getting spooked and killing her. He gave himself away when he made up that story about passing by the barn and the car not being there, which I'm still not sure why he did—just a psychological tell or a way of trying to confuse us even more—but there was no way that car was moved after it was backed into the side of that barn. Between the time Lance Stephenson saw it and the highway patrol the next morning, it didn't move. It couldn't. But he said it had. My guess is he distracted Lina and Kimmy—had them looking in a different direction when they passed the barn—but it could've just worked out that way."

We turned off the highway onto the dirt road that winds along part of the river on the way to Alabama Landing.

The sandy surface of the road was damp and dotted with small puddles from an early evening rainstorm.

The moon was low and large, its reflection refracted in the hundreds of coffee-with-creme-colored mud puddles and the millions of raindrops on the grass and trees.

As we pulled up in front of the large, crumbling, old two-story hunting lodge, I put the car in park and shook my head at what I was seeing.

Before we had left town, I stopped by the convenience store and used the pay phone to call the Oasis.

Lina had answered.

"Hey, Lina, it's John. I was gonna come by and give you and Kenny an update and ask a few more questions. Y'all both there tonight?"

"Just like always," she'd said. "The Bobbsey Twins are in action. Or inaction. Not much happening here tonight."

"I'll be by a little later," I'd said. "Y'all mind hanging out until I can get there?"

"Not a problem."

"Cool. See you then."

Now in the car Merrill was shaking his head as he looked at the decrepit old lodge. "This shit got a name? 'Cause if it ain't House of Usher, it missin' an opportunity."

I cut the engine and we studied the ancient, sagging structure, which looked pale and haunted in the moonlight.

The house looked abandoned, its seemingly empty interior shrouded in darkness.

All of the upstairs windows were dark

and only one downstairs showed even a hint of illumination.

"Make sense that the mom would stay on the first floor," Merrill said.

"Be nice if she's already in bed for the night," I said.

"Yeah, I ain't wantin' to eighty-six an old white lady in her PJs if I don't have to. 'Course . . . he did what you think he did and she raised his evil ass to do it . . . may not be a bad thing."

We climbed out of the air-conditioned car into the hot, humid night and eased down the dirt driveway beneath a canopy of huge oak trees, their limbs laden with Spanish moss.

The moist, sandy surface of the drive was moon-dappled, its granules clinging to our shoes.

Forcing the back door as quietly as we could, we entered the dim house to find the interior in worse shape than the exterior.

Maybe Kenny had chosen the barn because it subconsciously reminded him of home.

Long hallways and high ceilings, shiplap walls and ornate crown molding—all going to rack and ruin, the entire old estate slouching toward the earth.

In the dim dustiness I saw old furniture draped in sheets and gaudy old wallpaper peeling off the walls.

In the dark distance, water dripped in wet thuds that echoed loudly through the lodge.

Merrill and I both clicked on our flashlights and began to make our way through what felt as much like Satis House from *Great Expectations* as the House of Usher to me.

Splitting up to search the place quicker, I took the stairs to the second floor while he headed into the long hallway leading down the east wing.

Following the narrow beam of my small flashlight, I looked up and down the hallway several times before beginning to go door to door.

Twisting the old rusty knobs, I pushed each creaking door open and looked inside, second-guessing my choice to no longer carry a sidearm.

Many of the rooms were completely empty. Others were filled with storage boxes.

A few had the kinds of things you'd find in an old attic—dust and cobweb-covered items that were old but not antique, in varying stages of incremental decay, not unlike the house itself.

As I neared the end of the hallway I could see that the door at the very end was not only less dusty than all the others but had a hasp and padlock on it.

My pulse quickened and I prematurely pictured Colby and Cody being reunited with their mom.

I began thinking back to what I had seen in the storage room that I might use to pry the hasp off the door.

After remembering a short length of galvanized pipe propped against the far wall, I turned to go retrieve it—and found myself staring right into the barrel of a stainless steel revolver.

The beam of my light gleamed on the barrel and then onto the crazed face of Kenny St. John beyond.

"Surprise," he said.

"Kenny," I said.

"Every other time you came by to talk to Lina and me you just came by," he said.

"You didn't call to make sure we were there. Where else would we be? I knew something was up the moment Lina told me."

I nodded. "Amateur mistake," I said. "I'm a little rusty."

"That little bit of rust cost you your life," he said.

"Is she still alive?" I asked.

"Of course," he said. "What good is she to me dead?"

"She trusted you," I said. "Confided in you."

"You have any idea how unguarded women are around a man they believe is gay?" he asked.

"Is she behind that door?" I asked. "Would you please let me take her to see her kids?"

"No, but I'll tell you what I *will* do," he said. "After I've buried your body in the swamp, I'll go and get her kids too, so we can be a complete family. Won't be long before that daughter of hers can be of service to me."

Just then Merrill stepped out of the dark and pointed his pistol at the side of Kenny's head. "I got somethin' you can service," he said.

Kenny froze.

Merrill said to me, "I was wrong about what story this house belong in. It's more Faulkner than Poe. Got a 'Rose for Emily' situation downstairs."

I took that to mean that Kenny's mom was dead in her bed downstairs, but if that was true then who answered the phone when Lina called?

"If he answered the phone as his mother the other night when Lina called, it's probably more Bates Motel than anything else."

"I didn't do it because I think I'm her," Kenny said. "I'm not crazy. I just like playing games and keeping up appearances."

"Your brain pan's about to make an appearance if you don't drop your gun," Merrill said. "No sudden movements. No movement at all except your hand releasing its grip on the gun and letting it fall to the—"

Before Merrill could finish what he was saying, Kenny shot himself in the face.

"—floor," Merrill said as Kenny's lifeless body crumpled onto it. "Want me to search his body for a key or shoot the lock off?"

"Let's leave him like he is for forensics," I said, "and shoot it off."

Rushing over to the locked door, I said, "Candace, if you can hear me, back away from the door. We're going to shoot the lock off. We're here to help you. Your children sent us. Kenny is dead and no longer a threat to you."

"Shit, man," Merrill said, "save something to tell her once we get this bitch open."

I stepped back and he stepped forward and placed the barrel of his pistol about an inch above the top of the lock. Then turning his head away, he squeezed the trigger. It took three shots but eventually the lock dropped to the floor not unlike Kenny.

Removing what was left of the lock, I pushed the door open, and we looked inside.

There strapped naked to a soiled bed was Candace, dehydrated and maybe a bit malnourished, but very much alive.

"Candace, I'm John and this is Merrill. We're here to help you. You are safe now. Colby and Cody hired us to find you."

"Hired?"

"Yes, but we don't expect to collect payment," I said. "We're gonna get you out of these restraints now, and you can put my shirt on."

I quickly took off my shirt as Merrill loosened the straps.

We each took a hand and helped her up and she put my shirt on.

"We're gonna get you out of here and to a hospital," I said.

"No," she said. "Just get me to my kids. All I care about is seeing them."

54

Later that night in the front yard of their no-longer-needed foster parent's house, Colby and Cody gave me some of the best hugs I had ever received.

It was perhaps the best outcome of any case I'd ever worked.

Candace was traumatized and would have to heal, but she was alive and Colby and Cody had their mom back.

Dad's department was taking care of the crime scene and handling the closing of the case as if Merrill and I had never been involved—something that was far easier to do since Kenny shot himself instead of making Merrill do it.

Not often, but occasionally, just occasionally, good triumphs over evil, bad men are put down, and children get their missing mom back.

It was almost enough to make me want to pick up my badge and gun again. Almost, but not quite. I wasn't quite ready for that yet, but for the first time in a long time, I thought I might actually be one day soon, and that was a certain type of progress I didn't take for granted. I didn't take it for granted at all.

"Thank you, John," Colby said. "Thank you for our mom."

WHEN I WALKED into my trailer, my phone was ringing.

"*Dude*," Kimmy said, "why didn't you take me with you to get Candace? If it's because I'm a girl—"

"If you don't know me better than that then—"

"I didn't think so, but— Why then?"

"You're a good cop, Kimmy," I said. "What I did was illegal. I broke into someone's home. I wasn't going to risk your career on a theory. I could've easily been wrong and Candace not even been there."

"You think I'm a good cop?"

"Yes, I do," I said. "Colby and Cody have their mom back tonight because of the work you did on this case."

"Well, I hope I helped some, but . . ."

"I'm telling you what you did was the most important part," I said. "You did all the official things I couldn't do, and you came up with all the valuable information we used to find her. Colby and Cody owe you more than they'll ever know."

"That's sweet of you to say, but you're the one who—"

"It's true. I mean it."

"Thank you. Anyway . . . I was going to call you tonight—even before I heard what happened and got so mad at you. Guess what I was doing while you were breaking and entering?"

"What's that?"

"Making my first arrest," she said.

"Really?"

"Guess who's sitting in one of our cells right now?"

"One of your exes?"

"Very funny," she said. "None other than Lance Stephenson. You were right. He's Creepy Carl *and* Velvet too. It's the same guy. And he has several outstanding warrants. He's a stalker and harasser of women in three states."

"And you got him off the street," I said. "Well done you."

"How'd you know the witness was the creeper?"

"I didn't. I just thought he might be and it'd be worth looking into."

"Well, you were right. But there's still one question we haven't answered."

"Just one?" I asked.

"Well, one I can think of at the moment. We don't know why Steve borrowed his neighbor's truck the night Candace went missing—or what he did with it."

"And we don't need to," I said. "It's not relevant to Candace's disappearance. There are always unanswered questions when a case gets cleared. Some that would've been answered if the case hadn't been solved when it was. Others that never would have."

"Yeah, I guess, but . . . I don't like it."

I didn't respond, and we fell quiet a moment.

"Savor this night," I said. "Not many like these. You helped get a missing mom back to her children and take a stalker off the board. Most cases don't have such good outcomes."

55

The Department of Corrections of the state of Florida incarcerated just under 60,000 inmates at a yearly cost of roughly 1.5 billion dollars. The number of people required to operate this department was 23,732.

I was among them once again.

It was an overcast Tuesday morning. I was sitting at my desk, having been reinstated thanks to the footage of the chapel incident and the relentlessness of FDLE agent Rachel Mills.

It was nice to be back at work. It was even nicer to see Daniels so disappointed at my return.

As I had expected, Stone and Daniels, and even Rachel Mills, agreed that all the tape showed was Skipper breaking up illegal activity.

A few members of the staff seemed genuinely glad to see me back, but most, like most of the inmates, were tentative and seemed reserved around me.

Mr. Smith was excited to see me. Well, as excited as he ever gets.

He said he knew I was innocent and was hoping Skipper wouldn't kill me. I had hoped that myself, still did in fact. What I didn't say, because I was trying not to think about it, was that someone else already had.

I called Laura to tell her the good news. She was, at the same time, happy for me and scared too.

I was headed down to tell Anna in person—and to talk to her about the case—when I opened my door and saw Officer Charles Hardy standing there.

"I'm sorry it's taken me so long to see you, sir," he said. "Several people told me you wanted to talk to me about the morning Johnson was killed, but I've been out of town. I'm in the reserves, and they sent us to help with some hurricane damage in Charleston."

Charles Hardy was an excellent correctional officer. His crisp uniform and patent-leather shoes showed his military training, as did his comfort with authority. From all appearances and reports he accepted the authority of those above him with honor and never abused the authority he was given over others.

"I really appreciate you stopping by. I realize this is not your shift, and you don't have to talk with me. I'm looking into this very unofficially."

"I understand, sir," he said. "I'll answer any questions you have."

"Thank you," I said. "But please call me John. I was just about to walk down to Classification. If you're headed that way we could talk while we walk."

"Yes, sir," he said. "That'd be fine."

We walked down the asphalt road of the upper compound. We were alone. It was still early. The inmates hadn't been released from the dorms yet.

"In the early morning hours of Tuesday, two weeks ago from today, two inmates started fighting in the infirmary," I said. "We've been told you were away from your desk and that Captain Skipper had to come break them up."

He nodded.

"Where were you?" I asked.

"I'm surprised they didn't tell you," he said. "When Captain Skipper came into the infirmary, he sent me to Confinement to pick up an incident report. When I got back, he was gone. Nurse Strickland told me that Captain Skipper had left word for me to take Jacobson to Confinement. So I turned right around and went back to Confinement, this time with Jacobson in tow. Strange thing was he made me fill out the DR. I wasn't there. Didn't witness it, but I had to write the report. I didn't want to, but I did it. I know how to follow an order. Later, when everything went down in the sally port, I was glad that I was not in the infirmary just before it happened."

"What time did you get back to the infirmary that morning?" I asked.

"I didn't," he said. "I was in Confinement until a few minutes before seven. When I walked back up to Medical, Officer Straub was about to go in to begin his shift. I gave him a report of the night's events. He went in. I walked up front."

"Who else was in the medical building that night?" I asked.

"Johnson and Jacobson, Nurses Anderson and Strickland, the orderly, Jones . . . and another inmate was there for a while." He tilted his head back and closed his eyes to concentrate on recalling the nearly forgotten name. "Thomas. Anthony Thomas was there for a while, and that's it. Oh and Captain Skipper. He's everywhere."

MORE THAN ANYTHING, including the case, I wanted to talk to Anna about contracting the infection, but I just couldn't. Not yet.

So we talked about the case, about all that had happened, what it meant, who might be behind it.

"So you don't think Skipper killed Johnson or Maddox?" she said.

I shook my head.

"Why?"

"Neither death benefits him. Maddox was his best customer. Johnson was his best product. He was making his own kind of killing on the little arrangement, so there was no reason for him to do any killing. It'd be putting an end to a serious paycheck."

"Maybe they were going to tell."

"I don't think so. Maddox wouldn't, because it was his secret too. A secret that he more than anyone wanted to keep quiet. He would've lost everything. And Johnson's an inmate. Nobody would believe him, and he didn't seem to mind it too much. He was being treated like a king—drugs, alcohol, no work, no trouble."

"There's always the possibility of a motive that we can't see."

"There's always that, but . . . If it were just motive, that would be one thing, but it's means, as well. If someone like Skipper wanted to kill an inmate, he wouldn't do it in the garbage truck. He'd do it by having him killed on the rec field or shot during an escape attempt or beaten to death in Confinement."

"Like he tried with you."

"Exactly," I said. "But there's more. All but one of the murders were particularly bloody, and the third would've been. I think

Skipper interrupted that one. They were all stabbed and disfigured. It's personal, not business. A business kill is dispassionate. A single gunshot wound to the back of the head. But stabbings, beatings, cutting, knives, blood, pain, that's personal."

"So who do you think did it?" she asked.

"Someone who has a very personal stake in all of this," I said. "This is about love that's been twisted into hate, not money or a cover-up. Unless, of course, it was made to look like something it wasn't."

"You think all the brutality could be a cover?"

I shrugged. "Could be, but it feels like what it is—twisted love, dark passion, revenge. Because even when something is made to look like something it's not, it usually still feels like what it really is. When Molly Thomas was explaining why she had made the accusation against me, that she'd do anything for Anthony, I thought about how much love and devotion was wrapped up in what she did. She loved him so much. I think that's the key."

"You don't think Molly had it done, do you?" she said. "She could have hired someone to do it, then gotten killed by him."

"Takes us back to Skipper again."

"Everything in this case does, doesn't it?"

AFTER LEAVING ANNA'S OFFICE, I walked out into the waiting room.

A couple of the men nodded at me.

I nodded back.

A few others were so were engrossed in paperbacks they never looked up.

I recognized Zane Gray, Robert B. Parker, and Stephen King.

As I started to walk out of the building, I heard the faint tapping of an electric typewriter coming from behind the door to Medical.

Turning back around, I pulled out my keys and opened the door.

Standing next to the storage room where the typewriter was, Nurse Anderson jumped when I opened the door. The door to the storage room was parted slightly, and she moved in front of it.

"Chaplain," she said as the typing stopped. "How are you?"

"Who's in there?" I asked.

She looked puzzled. "Where do you—"

I pushed past her and opened the door.

Inside, Allen Jones was stuffing a sheet of typing paper into his pants pocket. I reached out and ripped it from his grip, tearing the corner as I did.

One glance let me know it was another letter warning and threatening me. I looked at Jones.

He was looking down at the floor, his weary shoulders slumped forward, his head downcast. "I's just trying to protect her," he mumbled.

Nurse Anderson appeared behind me. "What's this all about? What is that?"

"Another piece of the puzzle," I said, and walked out of the room.

"Chaplain, wait," she called after me. "You don't understand. I was only—"

56

That night, alone and lonely, I focused the full weight of my attention on the case, the crimes, the murders.

I was sore and aching, but thought better when I moved around, so paced up and down the length of my trailer as I went over everything.

Something was bothering me, needling a small spot of my subconscious with the irritation at the frustrating edge of my memory like a name once known but now forgotten.

Before finally giving in to pacing and thinking, I had tried to do many things when I came home after work—among them, watching the local news, reading, cooking, anything—but nothing worked but bumping around my trailer.

As I paced through the tight quarters I was temporarily calling home, I occasionally careened off the thin walls and the cheap furniture, the pain further focusing my thoughts and attention.

As I walked and thought and ricocheted around my rooms, I wondered how Molly's death figured into the others. Skipper most likely killed her in order to keep her quiet. She was the only one who could link him to all of the crimes he was involved in, and she had nothing to lose by telling all. Nothing to lose, that was, except her life.

The thought at the edge of my consciousness slowly drifted in. I saw the stack of videotapes, images of Maddox, Johnson, and Thomas flickering on the screen.

What was it? What had I missed when I previewed the tapes?

I walked over and pulled the tapes out of the linen closet. I placed them on the floor in front of the TV stand and pulled the chair over in front of the TV.

I turned on the TV and VCR and pushed

the first tape in. As it began to play, the images that had been floating around in my head the past few days filled the screen, accompanied by the tape's dull moans of both pleasure and pain.

I tried to watch other parts of the screen this time, forcing myself to look away from that which most drew attention to itself in each frame. Nothing. I did this with all the tapes, and still nothing.

I sat there staring at the TV screen, now playing the late news. The anchorperson was saying that Molly's car accident was believed to be suicide. She went on to say how distraught Molly had been over the death of her husband, an inmate incarcerated at PCI.

I wasn't really listening to her, though. I was still trying to think of what I had missed. I was sure it was on one of the tapes.

What had it been?

And then it hit me like a tire iron across the face. I jumped up and ran toward my bedroom, bumping into the walls of the narrow hallway as I went. I retrieved the other tape—the eight-millimeter one—from the drawer in my bedside table and ran back into the living room, where the light was better.

We had started a video recording production service at my church in Atlanta. Having a limited budget to begin with, we used Hi8 tapes and equipment and did most of the work ourselves.

I learned a lot about video production during that time. One of the things I learned was that it is best to fast forward a new tape all the way to the end and then rewind it to the beginning before starting to record on it. This caused all of the loose magnetic particles on the tape to drop off so there'd be fewer fade-outs during recording and playback.

Of course, most people didn't practice this technique.

On the tapes that hadn't been fast-forwarded to the end and then rewound to the beginning before being used for recording, it was obvious how much of the tape had been recorded on. This was because once the tape had been rewound, the part that had been used was not level with the part that hadn't on the spool. This was because the tape that had been used was looser and uneven, whereas the tape that was unused was still wound tight and smooth.

As I looked at the eight-millimeter tape from Maddox's collection, I could tell that an amateur had done the recording. Over half of the tape was loose and uneven, while the other half was smooth and tight. This meant that only half of the tape had been used before it was rewound. This also meant that an hour of footage was on the two-hour tape. An hour had been recorded, but we had only viewed a few minutes. There was more footage on the tape. I had let the tape play some after the scene had ended but now I wondered if I hadn't waited long enough for the next scene to come on.

There was one way to find out.

Uncle Tyrone's eight-millimeter VCR was still at the prison in the conference room next to Stone's office where I had used it to show him and Daniels the footage of Anthony and Molly Thomas in the chapel.

Unable to carry everything given how I was feeling, I had left the VCR and just brought home the tapes in order to protect them.

I raced to the prison and parked in front of Admin.

One of only two buildings outside the fence, I was able to enter Admin through the front door without checking in or being seen by the control room.

Rushing down the dark corridor in only the tiny red glow from the Exit sign above the door on the far end, I entered the conference room and turned on the TV and the eight-millimeter VCR still hooked to it.

Like the rest of the building, the conference room was dark and quiet, the occasional creaks of the structure and the hum of the central air the only sounds.

I put the tape in and pushed the fast forward button.

After passing through the chapel scene at rapid speed, the screen turned to white noise and then to blue. I continued to fast forward it. In about three minutes, an image appeared on the screen again.

The infirmary at night. The camera positioned in the hallway outside, shooting through the windows.

Johnson and Thomas. No Jacobson. Both on the far wall. Three beds in between them.

The screen turned to snow and then blue again.

Before I could hit the fast forward button, another image flickered on.

It was a close-up of Johnson and Thomas having violent sex together on one of the beds in between them. They looked like animals, gnawing and pawing at each other. I saw no evidence of love or affection. Both men were drunk or high or both.

In another minute, Sandy Strickland entered the room and caught them. She walked right up to where they were before they knew she was there.

No sound could be heard from inside the infirmary, but there was plenty of sign language.

She raged at Anthony. It was obvious that she cared for him, that she was hurt by what she had just seen. The look on her face was undiluted disgust.

Anthony at first bowed his head and looked like a wounded little boy, but as she continued to berate him, something changed.

He glanced over at Johnson for his response to the whole scene, and that set him off.

He pulled back and punched Sandy hard in the stomach.

She bent over and stepped back. Within seconds, Johnson was behind her forcing her down on the bed.

It was difficult to watch but I didn't look away—even as my pounding heart filled with pain and nausea spread through me.

They ripped her clothes off and began to beat and rape her.

The violence and brutality was even more surreal because it was silent.

Even more disconcerting and discordant were the expressions on the two men's faces. As they beat and brutalized her, they smiled and laughed wickedly.

The entire attack took less than ten minutes, but in those sadistic six hundred seconds, both Thomas and Johnson had raped, beaten, and sodomized Sandy Strickland.

Molly Thomas and Sandy Strickland. Skipper had made his own little rape tape. I could tell that the second rape had actually occurred before the first one—Jacobson wasn't in the infirmary like on the night of the murder, and Sandy Strickland wore the old gray nurse's uniform that had since been abandoned by the department for something a little brighter.

Skipper must have recorded a lot of footage during the first rape that he deemed unworthy or that somehow showed him and so recorded over it.

As I continued to watch, a couple of things caught my eye.

At some point near the end, a door opened into the hallway where the camera was positioned.

I rewound the tape and played the same footage again. This time when the door opened and the light poured into the hallway, I pushed the pause button.

There he was.

When the light came into the dark hallway, it made the glass the camera was shooting through reflect the image like a mirror, revealing that the cameraman was Matt Skipper.

Just over his right shoulder, standing just behind Skipper in the doorway to the caustic storage room, was the inmate orderly Allen Jones.

57

The veil of darkness covering the compound seemed much more than only the absence of light.

I was alone in the pervasive darkness. I was in it and it was in me. Or so it seemed.

I had entered the institution just a few minutes before.

"Everybody's working late tonight," the control room officer said.

"Who else?"

"That tall, pretty classification officer. Medical called her in on an emergency transfer."

My heart started racing.

I spun around and quickly scanned the parking lot.

There in the employee parking lot was Anna's car.

"Who's the OIC?" I asked.

"Captain Skipper."

I shook my head and frowned.

"What is it, Chaplain?"

"Will you call Sergeant Monroe and ask him to meet me in Medical?" I said, rushing down the compound before he responded.

The daytime noise and movement of inmates and officers was replaced by the eerie silence and lonely stillness of night.

When I reached the medical building, the officer's desk was vacant.

I walked down the hallway past the nurses' station where an elderly nurse dozed with her head on the counter.

I continued toward the infirmary to find that there was no officer stationed here either. There were no inmates in the infirmary so there was no need for an officer.

When I walked into the infirmary, I saw Sandy Strickland sitting alone on an exam stool beside one of the beds. Her upper body was slumped down on the bed, her right hand extended, rubbing the bed gently. I could hear her crying from the moment I entered the room.

As I approached, she jerked up, looked puzzled, and began wiping her eyes.

"What the hell are you doing here?" she asked.

"I just came from viewing a videotape of what Thomas and Johnson did to you here in this very room."

"I don't know what you're talking about," she said nervously. "What video? What do you mean?"

"I mean Skipper recorded it. Thomas and Johnson assaulting you."

She began to cry and I could tell she was on something. Something strong.

"Oh my God," she said. "He could've stopped it. That sick . . . prick. He just watched . . . stood there filming as they . . ."

"I understand why you'd want to kill them," I said, "but why not just turn them in. Why not let the—"

"I didn't want Anthony punished. I loved him. I just wanted him free of that little nigger faggot and that fat bastard banker faggot. They turned him into . . . He used to be

so . . . They infected him. Fucked . . . HIV . . .
right into his . . . Gave him AIDS. Then he
gave it to me. Or maybe it was Johnson. I . . .
I'm . . . I'm dying. Fucker killed me too. I'm
dying. Me. Not you. You're not.I . . . I gave you
my results, not yours. I was just so . . ."

The room around us, the building
around it, was still and night-quiet.

"I blamed you," she said. "Blame everybody . . . at this fuckin' place. Y'all are all part
of the . . . Skipper's the worst but . . . you're all
to blame. All you pricks stick together—
when you're not sticking each other."

"Sandy, I want you to come with me," I
said. "Let's go talk to . . . some people who
can help. Let's go tell them what you did to
Anthony and the others. I'm sure they'll understand. I'm sure they'll help you."

She looked confused. "I didn't do anything to Tony. I could never . . . I loved him.
Took care of those other two buttfucks to
protect him. I didn't . . . I could never . . . hurt
him. I . . . I'll hurt everybody . . . else here . . .
you . . . all of . . . but not him. I'm . . . not goin'
to . . . talk to . . . any . . . I've got that nosy
bitch from Classification . . . you're so . . . in . .
. I'll kill her. I'll slice her open."

She spun around on her stool to the bed behind her, pulling off the sheet to reveal Anna, bound and gagged and crying.

When Anna saw me a quick flash of relief danced in her eyes. But it didn't last long. Her eyes filled with terror again when Sandy pulled the scalpel from her pocket and placed it at Anna's throat.

"So . . . pretty . . . So . . ."

"Sandy, no, please. Don't—"

She pressed the knife hard against Anna's throat.

Sandy had obviously administered some sort of paralytic or something because Anna didn't move or scream as blood began pouring out of the small opening on the right side of her neck.

"Miss Sandy, you okay?" Allen Jones asked as he stepped into the infirmary.

Walking over toward her, he glanced at Anna with neither expression nor comment.

I had to come up with something quick, but what? How long did Anna have?

I thought about Sandy saying she hadn't killed Anthony, that she loved him and would never—

"You didn't kill Anthony, did you?" I said.

She looked back at me. "I told you . . . I wasn't even . . . here . . . when it . . . happened. Oh God, I want him back."

The blood was flowing more freely from Anna's neck now.

"In a way you did kill him," I said.

"What . . ."

"Your love for him got him killed. He was killed by someone who loves you."

"What . . . Who?"

"Him," I said, gesturing toward Jones.

I could see the look of realization as the truth of what I'd said dawned on her.

"He was watching that night," I said. "I've seen the video. He can be seen just behind Skipper, watching what they did to you. He was going to kill them all but you beat him to Johnson and Jacobson's been in Confinement, but Thomas . . . When his wife got him released from Confinement . . . he . . . did to him what he had done to you—only with a scalpel."

She looked over at Jones with utter contempt.

"You . . . *stupid* . . . useless . . . What did you do? What did you think? That . . . *you* . . . had a shot. I loved him, not you. Never you.

He was my *everything*. You are nothin' to me. A worthless ... old ... You mop the floors for fuck sake. You ..."

She started toward him with the scalpel.

When she reached him, she brought up the weapon, but slapped him first hard across the face with her open hand.

He didn't flinch.

She swiped at his face with the scalpel, slicing his cheek open, his blood beginning to pour out and join Anna's on the floor.

And then it happened.

In one quick motion, he wrapped his huge hands around her small throat and broke her neck.

As her body went limp, he took the scalpel from her and stabbed her several times in the heart, then slit her throat.

Her head fell to the side unnaturally, and as he let her go, she crumpled to the floor.

Spinning around, he started to rush me.

Just before he reached me, I snapped out a hard right jab square on his nose. It stunned him, and blood started pouring out of it.

Staggering back a step or two, he righted himself and came again. This time ducking his head down and tackling me. As he did, the scalpel clanged on the floor a few feet away.

Still sore and aching, my entire body screamed with pain as I hit the floor.

Get to Anna. Hurry. You've got to hurry.

On top of me now, he began to flail at me wildly, hitting my left eye and chin and shoulder and arm.

I brought my midsection up, rocked forward, then back, and bucked him off. Jumping to my feet, I began to rush over to Anna's bed, once white, now crimson.

Climbing to his feet, Jones had the scalpel in his hand again.

"Think what I gonna do to her after I gut you," he hissed.

I braced for his attack but it never came.

About halfway to me, his feet flew out from underneath and he hit the floor hard. He had slipped on all the blood—Anna's, his, Sandy's.

As he attempted to find purchase in the slippery fluid, Merrill rushed into the room, an officer's baton in his hand.

I ran over to Anna as Merrill went toward Jones.

Jones reached his feet, his eyes wild and wide, and ran at Merrill.

Scalpel extended, rabid expression on his face, Jones hurled himself toward Merrill.

At first it looked as if Merrill wasn't doing anything or had waited too late to defend himself, but just as Jones was on him, he brought the baton up into his chin then down on his falling head.

The blows were fast and furious and Jones stopped dead, but didn't go down.

Merrill lifted the baton again and brought it back down across the left side of his face.

His whole head jerked back and blood and teeth spewed out as he collapsed to the floor.

"Anna's cut," I said. "Bleeding out. We've got to get her to a hospital."

"We *in* a hospital. I'll grab some help."

He dashed out of the room.

I pressed the wound on Anna's neck, feeling for a pulse as I did.

"Anna. Anna. Hey. Open your eyes. Anna, it's John. I . . . Please wake up. Please open your eyes. Anna."

In a few moments Merrill rushed back in with medical personnel and a doctor.

"She's lost a lot of blood," the doctor said.

"We have the same blood type," I said. "Give her mine."

"Are you absolutely positive?"

"Yes," I said, "and it's disease free. I was just tested."

I climbed on the table beside her, her blood soaking into my clothes, and the doctor quickly found a vein, transferring my blood into her body as he worked on her wounds and called for an ambulance. Her blood had helped save me. Now my blood— my clean, virus-free, life-giving blood— would do the same for her. I was sure of it.

58

A few days later, I was seated on the edge of Anna's hospital bed, the afternoon sun streaming in through the open blinds striping the bed and warming the room.

The door was closed. We were alone.

Anna was wearing an oversized cotton nightshirt with bouquets of violets against a soft yellow background. Her hair hung straight down to the smattering of dark freckles just above her breasts and had the fluffy look of having just been blown dry.

The bandage on her neck was smaller than the one the day before, and when we had hugged, I had smelled the slightest hint of her perfume.

"Your blood's in my veins," she said.

I nodded. "I keep thinking about that."

"Me too."

We fell silent a moment.

"You never told me what brought you to the infirmary," she said.

I told her.

"Did you suspect Strickland before you saw the tape?"

I nodded. "She was the first to appear at the scene that Tuesday morning in the sally port when Johnson was killed. She was there before Medical was called. I think she wanted to make sure Johnson actually got killed. If he'd just been injured, she could finish the job. And that's exactly what she did. She smashed his windpipe. She was the only one who could have. She climbed onto the back of that truck not as a healer, but a killer."

"How'd she do it? Get him in the bag in the back of the truck in the first place."

"She had Hardy take Jacobson to Confinement so she could drug and dispose of Johnson. She put him in the caustic storage room, then locked it so Jones couldn't get in. Then she spilled a urine sample in the exam room and had Anderson supervise Jones cleaning it up. When Shutt pulled up and knocked on the door, she didn't answer it. When he walked over to Laundry, she carried the bags out and put them in his truck."

She nodded, squinting slightly. I could tell that she was picturing everything I was saying.

"Of course, when I saw the video, I knew it had to be her and then I also knew why. And it doesn't mean as much as it once did, but poison is historically a woman's method of murder. Both of her victims were poisoned or drugged. The violence was never direct."

"Was for Anthony Thomas. What about him?"

"I suspected Jones of being involved too. I knew he'd typed the letters to me and Johnson's request threatening suicide or escape. I didn't think Strickland had killed Anthony Thomas—and not only because she was in love with him but because it was direct, brutal violence."

"Yeah, she saved that shit for me."

"She was disintegrating fast by then. I think she had some torture planned for Maddox, had two of his knives ready for it after she drugged him, but Skipper banging on the door with Thomas made her cut things short."

"How about Molly Thomas? Who killed her?"

"I think Skipper did it, but I can't prove it."

"So Skipper had a prostitution ring, sold drugs, had you beaten up, and has maybe murdered someone, and he gets away with it?"

"For a little while longer maybe," I said. "He's being investigated. Word's out on the compound, so . . ."

59

I was standing at the gate of Potter Correctional Institution staring at him when he was killed.

It was Monday morning of the following week.

Thick clouds had rolled in during the night, replacing the sunny skies of the weekend, the gray day matching the buildings of the institution.

In the sally port, Merrill Monroe was stabbing trash bags with an iron rod on the back of a flatbed truck, his graceful, fluid motion a thing of beauty.

Seeing me at the gate, he paused and waved.

"Somebody say somethin' 'bout me bein' a spear-chucker . . . I'a show 'em why my ancestors called that."

I started to say something but stopped as the most powerful sense of déjà vu washed over me.

When Merrill stabbed the next bag, the rod stuck and wouldn't give as he attempted to withdraw it.

On his second, more strenuous attempt, Merrill was able to snatch the weapon free, but it came out of his hands and went flying through the air.

Striking the fence nearest me, it splattered the steel and concrete with blood.

Merrill looked at me, slowly shaking his head in disbelief, as the officer in the control room buzzed me through the two gates that separated us.

I rushed over to the vehicle in what felt like a recurring nightmare and climbed onto it with Merrill.

A small pool of blood was seeping outward from the bag.

Bending over, I pulled open the bag, peeling back the sides, the wet plastic slipping from my grip, the warm blood bathing my fingers, as it opened to reveal the lifeless, bloody body of Captain Matthew Skipper, his vacant eyes filled with far more peace in death than they ever had been in life.

I looked back at Merrill, wondering if he'd had anything to do with this beyond what I'd just witnessed.

His opaque expression was implacable. "Kinda poetic, ain't it?"

I nodded.

"Jacobson got out of Confinement over the weekend," he said.

I stood and turned to look down toward the compound.

Beyond the medical and security personnel running in this direction, a small group of inmates had gathered in front of the center gate. There in the midst of them, straining to see along with the others, was Jacobson, a wide grin seeping across the wild expression on his pale face.